HARTSVILLE'S SEAL HEROES

The SEAL's Convenient Wife

The SEAL's Surprise Baby

The SEAL's Instant Family

The SEAL's Pregnant Roommate

The SEAL's Treatment

The SEAL's Hookup

This is a work of fiction. Names, characters, places and incidents either are the product of imagination or are used fictitiously. Any resemblance to actual persons, living or dead, events or locales, is entirely coincidental.

Leslie North is a pen name created by Relay Publishing for co-authored Romance projects. Relay Publishing works with incredible teams of writers and editors to collaboratively create the very best stories for our readers.

Cover Design by Mayhem Cover Creations.

www.relaypub.com

THE SEAL'S *Instant Family*

HARTSVILLE'S SEAL HEROES BOOK THREE

USA TODAY BESTSELLING AUTHOR

LESLIE NORTH

BLURB

Navy SEAL Kenton Fitzpatrick has his life planned out. Retire from the military in a few years, find a lovely woman, get married, have kids. But all that gets thrown off when he comes home from a mission ahead of schedule and finds a beautiful woman with toddler twins and a slobbery dog living in his house. Mia Kingston, who gained custody of her nieces when her sister died, lost her apartment in a fire, so Kenton's mom thought it would be fine for her to stay in his house while he was deployed. Though having a family living with him isn't ideal, Kenton agrees to let them stay. With his life plan set in stone, he has no worries that a free spirit like Mia will throw him off track. But when an enemy from Kenton's past surfaces looking for revenge—and puts Mia and the twins in his sights—Kenton may have to accept a change in plans.

Mia always intended to return to her apartment once repairs were completed. And she never intended to fall for a sexy SEAL. Then again, even with the chaos of the twins, the threats on their lives, and Kenton's frustrating need to plan *everything*, Mia's never been happier. Having lost her parents at a young age, it's nice to have a family—even if it's not quite real. While Kenton's focused like a laser on keeping them all safe, Mia's struggling to keep her heart safe from falling too hard, too fast.

Will it take nearly losing Mia for Kenton to realize he can't live without her?

MAILING LIST

Thank you for reading "The SEAL's Instant Family"
(Hartsville's SEAL Heroes Book Three)

Get SIX full-length novellas by USA Today best-selling author Leslie North for FREE! Over 548 pages of best-selling romance with a combined 2748 FIVE STAR REVIEWS!

Sign-up to her mailing list and get your FREE books:

www.leslienorthbooks.com/sign-up-for-free-books

CONTENTS

1

─────

Kenton Fitzpatrick closed his laptop and eyed the men who sat across from him. Patrick and Anderson were integral members of the SEAL team he captained—and his two closest friends.

"I'm not satisfied with what happened," he said with a shake of his head. The higher-ups weren't pleased with his team's performance, either, so he'd taken some heat. Not something he was accustomed to. "I want a do-over."

The mission to North Africa to take down a child-trafficking ring had been at best partially successful. Kenton's team had managed to disrupt, but not destroy, the network that brought in children from all over the world and sent them back out to fates he didn't want to contemplate.

"Not likely for us," Patrick said, leaning back in his chair. "But another team will get assigned to finish what we didn't."

"Maybe they'll have better luck," Anderson said.

"Luck has nothing to do with this kind of work," Kenton said flatly. He snatched a pen off the table and clicked it while he thought. It was true that occasionally his SEAL team caught a break, but success came from meticulous planning and flawless execution. He excelled at the former and was well known for it. And he couldn't fault his men's actions. They'd done what he'd planned, but the trafficking ring's leader had slipped through their grasp. Kenton didn't think it would be long before Marcus Ocampa built another network to prey on innocent children. And that pissed him off.

"I'm still trying to sort out exactly where it went wrong," Anderson said. His language skills and analytical brain had been invaluable during the mission, but nothing had been enough to get the team to their end goal.

"Me, too." Kenton needed to think about it more, mull it over. Maybe then it would come to him. He wanted to know what his mistakes had been, so he could avoid them in the future. "I appreciate you guys sticking around to help me finish up." Anderson and Patrick had stayed on base an additional two days, answering questions alongside him and helping him complete the reports when they could have gone home to their families.

"No worries. I can't imagine having one of my kids taken from me and exploited like that," Patrick said with a shudder. He was the father of an eight-year-old girl and a baby boy. "It makes me want to hold my kids close and never let them out of my sight."

Anderson nodded his agreement. He'd married just prior to deploying on this mission, and he and his wife already had a little boy.

"I'll bet your families are anxious to see you. Have you talked to them since we got stateside?" Kenton asked, feeling guilty that they'd lost out on time with their wives and kids.

"Early this morning. They're fine." Patrick grinned. "It'll be complete chaos when I get home."

"You love it," Kenton said.

"I do," Patrick was quick to say. "You'll have to try it sometime."

"I'll get there eventually." Kenton said. He had definite ideas about his future, and kids were part of it, he'd realized in recent months. He already had a house he loved. It was a recent purchase, but he felt sure it was the place where he'd bring his bride. First, he had to meet the right woman, and then, when the time was right, they'd have a couple of kids.

"Eventually is never how it happens," Anderson said with a laugh. "Some woman's going to burst into your plans and change everything."

"You got that right," Patrick agreed. "Just prepare yourself to catch her when she falls into your life, because you won't get any warning."

That seemed to be the way of it with his friends and SEAL teammates. Most had paired off in recent years and were busy raising families. Still, Kenton didn't think a woman was going to land on his doorstep like his buddies seemed to think.

"I've got to be home long enough for that to happen." If he wasn't deployed, Kenton advised other teams about to head out. It was a life that kept him out of the country or on base the majority of the time, which was why he was looking forward to heading home. He had an extended leave coming, and he planned to take it. He wanted to take care of some projects around the house, but his true goal was to lay the foundation for his future. And that meant finding a woman to share it with.

Kenton's phone screen lit up again with another message from his mother. Margaret Fitzpatrick was the most persistent woman he'd ever known. He'd texted her earlier in the day that he'd be headed home soon, and she'd sent him five messages since asking him to call.

"You should call or text your mom back," Anderson said, reading the screen from across the table. "You know how she is."

The three of them shared a grin. Margaret had been a mom to all of them since Patrick's had walked out when he was a kid, and Anderson's was never much interested in parenting. Margaret had been the one who made sure they all had Halloween costumes when they were little and got home from football practices in high school. She was a mother hen who didn't put up with any nonsense.

"Later," Kenton said. "She probably just wants to invite me to dinner. I'm not feeling it."

"You've got to let the mission go," Anderson said, standing up. "We've analyzed it. Viewed it from every angle. What happened wasn't your fault, man."

"I'm not convinced of that yet," Kenton said. The sense of responsibility stayed with him as they drove off base and headed for Hartsville. Kenton dropped off Patrick first, at his house just outside town, and watched as his friend was engulfed in hugs from his wife and kids. Next, he took Anderson to a home in a newer development. The porch light was on, and Violet immediately stepped outside with their son Nate on her hip and a huge smile on her face.

Kenton beeped his horn as he drove off, happy that his friends had each found a mate who suited them, even if both of them had fallen into relationships in unusual ways. A few minutes later, he turned onto the tree-lined street where he lived. He'd bought the home, sight unseen, eighteen months ago, when he was on the other side of the globe. He'd viewed pictures on the internet and had his family's assurance that he'd love it. And he did. More than he could put into words.

The dark blue Victorian was stately and graceful, the kind of place that exuded comfort and security. It was exactly what he wanted. Patrick and Anderson had teased him about the ornate trim, stained-glass transom window, and rounded turret. He'd taken the ribbing while thinking that his future wife, whoever she was, would appreciate those details.

As he pulled into his driveway, he was just glad to be there and have time and space to himself. He'd call his mom in the morning, but he wanted to sleep in his own bed first. Unpack and unwind before having to socialize. That was always best when he came off a mission. He needed time to adjust to the civilian world.

He grabbed his duffel bag, pausing when he heard a dog bark. He listened more closely. The twilight air was still and quiet, with only the hum of the cicadas and the slight puff of an early autumn breeze in the trees. He waited, and the bark came again. He could have sworn the sound was coming from inside his house, but his ears must be playing tricks on him. He loved dogs, had even gotten interested in training them in the military, but he hadn't owned one since he was a kid.

With a shrug, Kenton let himself into the mudroom and dropped the duffel on the floor. A scrabbling of paws on the tile floor was his only warning before a large dog slammed into him, knocking him off balance and pinning him to the wall. The dog's head was against Kenton's chest. It didn't move to bite him, but Kenton felt the heat of its breath and heard a low growl from its throat.

What the hell! What was a dog doing in his house?

Before Kenton could attempt to shove the dog away, a baseball bat was thrust into his side. Shit. Had he entered the wrong house somehow? His fist clamped around the key he still held. No, he'd let himself in. Before he could say anything, the pressure left his side as his attacker changed strategies and swung at his head. He parried instinctively and caught the bat before it connected, but he couldn't prevent the glancing hit to his shoulder.

He gripped the bat and wrenched it away from his assailant. At the same time, he pushed off the wall, shoving the dog back as his senses processed who he was up against. He squinted, trying to make out a shape in the shadows. The figure was not what he'd expected. Tall and curvy, the dip of her waist a defined valley between bust and hips. And he caught the faint whiff of perfume, fresh violet.

A woman? The realization made him hesitate. He'd have had a man on the floor in no time, but…

"What are you doing here?" The voice was feminine, pitched low and threatening. Kenton would be impressed with her bravery if he weren't so damn annoyed to find someone in his house.

"This is my house," he ground out. The dog retreated from him and went to her. "What the hell are *you* doing here?"

No answer came, but a blast of light from overhead illuminated the space. She'd flipped on the old fluorescent bulb that hung above them.

"Holy hell," he said under his breath when he caught sight of her.

She was gorgeous. Gold streaked her dark blonde hair, and her eyes were green like summertime leaves. A smattering of freckles covered her nose and cheekbones. And her mouth was a lush, deep pink, inviting and teasing his imagination. He hadn't been wrong about the curves, either. The swell of her chest beneath her tight-fitting shirt sparked a thirst within him that only seemed to grow as his eyes slid over her hips and down her long legs. The black leggings she wore hid nothing.

She wasn't eye level with him—few women were—but she was taller than average. The fleeting thought that she'd fit just right against his large frame came and went in his brain in the split second they evaluated each other.

Her chin came up, a look of challenge on her face, and she continued to hold the bat clutched in front of her, long lashes blinking over her eyes. He needed to speak, but he was still drowning in the sight of her.

Her lips parted, and before she could speak, the sharp cry of a child came from overhead. A kid? There was an unknown woman, a dog, *and* a kid in his house? What alternate universe had he walked into?

"Oh, damn," she muttered.

2

____

"**S**orry," Mia said.

She had recognized his face as soon as the light came on. Kenton Fitzpatrick, the home's owner. Pictures of him with his family or other men dressed in uniform lined the mantel. She'd studied those pictures, adored those pictures, and dreamed of having his tall, built frame around hers on more than one occasion. And the photos hadn't lied, he was all muscle with high cheekbones and a sharp jaw.

Dark hair, intense eyes, tanned skin, and the shadow of stubble—the man was a heartbreaker. No doubt about it.

His imposing attitude didn't detract, even a little bit, from his sensual, masculine persona. Except he looked confounded and pissed at the moment, since he was probably completely unaware that she was... well... living in his house.

She lowered the baseball bat, no longer worried about defending herself and her nieces, and grabbed for Eliot's collar. Tension still coiled through the dog, making it hard for her to drag him away from Kenton.

"Come on, Eliot. Be a good boy," Mia pleaded. The chocolate lab mix was usually the perfect family pet. Lovable and happy. But he didn't like anyone he perceived as a threat to her or the girls. An unknown man entering the house after dark was definitely more than he could handle. Mia gave another yank on his collar. "Down, Eliot. It's okay."

"I'm glad *you* think it's okay," Kenton said, his hands going to his hips. "From where I'm standing, someone has invaded my house."

"Right. About that…" She trailed off as she struggled with Eliot and with how to explain her presence in Kenton's beautiful home. Another piercing cry from upstairs cut through the air. Most likely Emma. She'd been unsettled all evening, so much so that Mia had been reluctant to put her in the room she shared with Ava, who was the quiet, calm twin. Emma, bless her little heart, was more demanding of attention. But Mia had thought she was tired enough to sleep. Eliot's barking must have woken her.

Mia felt torn between dealing with the dog, explaining her presence to her unexpected visitor, and racing up the stairs to comfort Emma before she woke her sister. She was on the verge of sprinting away when Kenton barked out a sharp command. She didn't recognize the language it was given in, but it had the immediate effect of making Eliot sit down and Emma stop crying.

What kind of wonder was this? Even Mia felt frozen in place.

Kenton's phone rang in the silence, but he made no move to answer it as his eyes swept over her from head to toe. His gaze was assessing, not critical, and she recognized interest in his eyes. The look disappeared as swiftly as it came.

"Are you going to answer that?" she asked, pulling out her own phone and opening the app that connected to the nanny cam in the twins' bedroom. Mia had only been a parent for six months, but she'd learned quickly that sudden silences were as terrifying as all-out screaming.

Emma's face showed on the small screen. The toddler was sitting in the corner of her crib with her favorite stuffed bunny on her lap. Tears glistened on her face as she chewed on the bunny's ear. She was okay. Mia took a deep breath. With any luck, Emma would settle herself back to sleep while Mia dealt with the angry man in front of her.

Kenton touched Eliot's ears and spoke in a low voice that Mia couldn't catch, but it was a tone the dog understood. He immediately pushed his nose into Kenton's hand and gave his wrist a lick. Eliot must have recognized the man's scent—it was all over the house, especially in the master bedroom.

Mia slept in the guest room herself, but she'd wandered into Kenton's bedroom from time to time, usually late at night after the girls were asleep. She'd been curious about the single man who'd bought such a lovely and large home. She hoped he'd never realize that she'd opened his closet and drawn in the rich scent of man and sandalwood from time to time.

Something about his scent and his belongings had felt reassuring to her at a time when her life was in chaos. Normally, she didn't mind a little uncertainty. She tended to thrive on it, but not now that she was responsible for her young nieces. She wasn't going to shed her free-spirited ways completely, but her priorities had had to shift.

"Would you like to explain to me why you're in my house?" Kenton asked, now that a subdued Eliot sat at his feet.

"I'm guessing you haven't had a chance to speak with your mom yet?"

"No." He narrowed his eyes. "Why?"

"Oh, she said she was going to get in touch with you." Mia had counted on Margaret explaining the situation to her son. Kenton's confusion and anger made more sense now. "Should we go into the living room to talk?" At his nod, she led the way, feeling odd as she walked through his house as if she were the hostess. "Sorry about the mess," she said with a quick glance around. When she'd moved in, the house had been immaculate, not a thing out of place. With two little kids, it was impossible to keep it that way. A basket of toys was turned over on the hardwood floor, a sippy cup sat on the cherrywood coffee table, and a discarded sweatshirt was draped on the sofa. The place wasn't ready for a *House Beautiful* photo shoot.

"I don't care about that," he said, but his shoulders tensed. He most certainly did care. She could see that as plain as day. "I want to know why you appear to live here and why there's a kid in my house."

"Two kids, actually." She hesitated, trying to decide the best way to contextualize her presence. "I guess it all started six months ago, when my sister and brother-in-law passed away in a car accident." Mia was proud of herself for getting the sentence out so calmly. Speaking of Caroline and Matt's deaths was still so hard. Her sister had been her one true friend, the rock that never shifted in her life, and she was taken away in the blink of an eye.

"I'm sorry," he said, gesturing for her to sit on the couch while he took a seat by the fireplace.

"They were hit from the side by a truck. The police told me they died instantly." She hoped that was the case, since she couldn't stand the thought of them suffering. "Fortunately, the girls were at the sitter's." The mix of emotions on the day of the accident had nearly killed her. She'd been so grieved about her sister but overjoyed Emma and Ava were okay.

"So you became their guardian?"

"Right. I don't have kids of my own. I mean… I'm not married or anything, so there was a learning curve. Parenting twins is tough." Mia had been a doting aunt since the girls were born, but that hadn't prepared her for being their full-time care provider. Her life had taken a radical shift.

"I'll bet. Now, about the house?" he prompted.

"I'm getting there," she said as another cry reached her from upstairs. She rose, unsure whether to dash off or stay and finish the story. She wanted him to understand, but she wasn't making progress toward that goal. "Anyway, about a month ago my apartment building caught fire—" A scream that climbed upward on the decibel meter came from Emma, and Mia jumped into motion. "I need to get her."

"But—" His phone's ring cut him off.

"Is that your mother?" Mia moved toward the stairs.

He shot her a look as he pulled his phone from his pocket and took a glance at the screen. "Yeah."

"Answer it, please. She'll explain." With that, Mia sprinted up the steps and headed toward the twins' room. "It's okay, baby," she said softly when she got to Emma's crib. The girl was sitting up, her eyes wide and her mouth open to yell again. Mia sucked in a breath. The twins looked so much like their mother, with their golden hair and brown eyes. Ava seemed to have her mother's personality, calm and thoughtful. Ava was a watcher. She wasn't docile, but she was patient.

"You're not, though, are you?" Mia spoke to Emma in a soft voice as she lifted her from the crib. "It's all 'Look at me, look at me' for you." After a quick peek to make sure Ava was still sleeping, Mia made her way back downstairs with Emma.

"All right, Mom, I get it," Kenton was saying into his phone. His broad back was turned, so he didn't see Mia enter the room. "They had nowhere else to go. Must have been a hell of a fire."

Mia shivered as she thought back to that night. The blare of the fire alarm had woken her at just past three. Normally, she wasn't someone who panicked, but as soon as she'd sat up, she'd smelled smoke. She'd flown out of bed, grabbing the first items of clothing she could find, and gone to the twins. Smoke swirled through her apartment, and she'd feared she wouldn't be able to make it down the stairs from the third floor. She'd wrapped both of them in damp towels and hoisted one girl on each hip before flinging her door open and racing for the stairwell with Eliot on her heels.

Once she'd gotten outside, Mia had hugged the babies to her and sat in the grass near her car, wondering what she was going to do, as the fire trucks arrived. The fire, pushed by a strong wind, raced through the building, damaging every unit. She kept repeating to herself that they were safe. Emma, Ava, Eliot—her little family was okay. Homeless and frightened but unharmed.

The local Red Cross had given her shelter for the night and food, but it was when she went to the bakery where she worked the following morning that she found her guardian angel in the form of Margaret Fitzpatrick. Margaret, who owned the clothing boutique next door to the bakery, had listened to the story of the fire and immediately suggested that Mia move into her son's home. Margaret had even helped Mia and the girls settle in, all the while insisting that Kenton would be deployed for several months yet.

But he'd arrived home early. Mia bounced Emma on her knee and tuned in to the conversation Kenton was having with his mother. Would he toss them out? She wouldn't blame him if he did. She rapidly considered her options. The company that owned her apartment building had another in the next town. But it was a forty-minute drive, and that building didn't allow dogs. What would she do with Eliot? And the long drive would really complicate her life.

"Why didn't you have them stay with you?" Kenton listened for a minute before responding. "That's right. I forgot you were remodeling." More silence on his end. "I didn't expect to be back yet, either, but I am." Kenton rubbed the back of his head as he spoke, making Mia realize how tired he must be and how he must have been looking forward to relaxing in his lovely, empty house.

Margaret hadn't filled in all the details about her son, but she'd said enough for Mia to know he was Special Forces and was often deployed all over the world. She wondered what kind of life that was and how it meshed with the traditional home he'd purchased. Somehow, it didn't seem to fit.

"Yeah, Mom, I'm fine. I'll come to dinner soon," he said in the tone of a man who wanted to end the conversation. "Tell Dad I said hello, and I'll see you."

Kenton hung up and turned, catching sight of her and Emma. She guessed by the hitch of his eyebrows that people didn't usually sneak up on him. Probably a sign of his exhaustion.

"This is Emma," she said and raised the toddler's hand in a wave. He studied the girl before cautiously lifting his hand to return her gesture.

"Cute kid," he said. "Are they identical?"

"Technically, yes, but they're easy to tell apart," she said. He nodded, and she noted the dark circles under his eyes. Time to wrap this up. "I guess your mom explained about the fire. She was sure you wouldn't be home, or I'd have never…"

"It's fine," he said, his hand rubbing the back of his neck again. "We'll figure out the details in the morning."

"I'm off tomorrow, so we can talk," Mia said. Her usual shift making bread, pastries, and doughnuts began early in the morning, which had proved challenging with the twins.

"Mom said you work at Hamman's Bakery." Kenton remained standing, making her wonder if he'd fall asleep instantly if he sat.

"That's how I know your mom." Mia had been reluctant to accept Margaret's offer of a place to stay. For herself, she never would have.

For the girls, she'd do what she had to.

"We'll talk in the morning," he said again. "I'm going to lock up and get some sleep." He moved toward the foyer but paused before leaving the living room. "Do you need any help? I mean, with…" He gestured to Emma.

"I've got it. Thanks, though." She listened to him moving through the house, checking the front door that she'd already locked and going through the kitchen to the mudroom to make sure it was secure. "Well, little girl," she said to Emma, whose eyes were looking heavy, "time for us to go to bed, too."

3

Kenton cracked his eyes open. He hadn't spent the night in his house often enough for it to feel familiar, but he liked the way the light reflected on the pale blue he'd painted his bedroom walls and the smell of pancakes cooking. It was homey.

Wait. Pancakes? He lifted his head off the pillow as memory hit him. He had guests. Was that the right word? Probably not. He had inhabitants. Before going to bed, he'd taken a few minutes to search online for an article about the fire that had left Mia homeless. Images of the blaze filled his screen, and he'd read the fire chief's comments about how it had been miraculous no one was killed when an apartment on the second floor caught fire.

Mia and her nieces were lucky to be alive, so Kenton could see why his mother had offered his house. The problem was that he'd been looking forward to being alone. He wanted some quiet time to reflect on his recent mission and to start mapping out his future. Both of those things were going to be difficult with a woman, two little kids, and an unruly dog in his space.

He heard a scratching sound on the door to his room, followed by a whine. A second later the door opened and Eliot bounded in, leaped straight onto Kenton's bed, and stood next to him.

"No," Kenton said, but the dog cocked his head to one side and licked Kenton's face. "Stop that." Kenton pushed at the dog's head, trying to get him to move away, but Eliot shook his head, causing his ears to flap and drool fly. And then, Eliot sneezed. Right on Kenton. "For god's sake. Get down, you beast."

Kenton sat up and managed to get the animal off the bed. "Now, sit," he commanded. Eliot wagged his tail and panted as if that was the correct response. "No one has trained you, have they?" Kenton let out a sigh. "We're going to have to work on that, after I have a conversation with your owner."

Kenton dug through his drawers and pulled on some clothes before following the scent of pancakes through the house. Eliot beat him to the kitchen, sliding across the floor and into Mia where she stood at the stove. She laughed when the dog licked her knee.

"Good morning, Eliot." Mia turned with the spatula in her hand to greet the dog and caught sight of Kenton in the doorway. "Good morning to you, too."

"Hi," he said, taking in the scene. The twins sat in high chairs that had been pulled up to the kitchen table. They were ripping apart pancakes and shoving chunks into their mouths. Kenton assessed the girls. Their features appeared to be identical. Exact same hair, eyes, and little noses. The only difference he could see was that one wore a blue shirt while the other had on purple. Both of them glanced up briefly. One met his gaze, but the other ducked her head and began eating again.

"Coffee is ready," Mia said, "and this pancake is just about to come out of the pan. It's in the shape of R2-D2, if you want to claim it."

She smiled at him. He'd only seen a hint of that the night before, or maybe he'd been too damn tired and shocked to notice. But it was bright enough to light a room.

"I have Mickey Mouse, too, if you prefer that." She gestured with her shoulder to the pancake on a plate nearby. "I do flowers, birds, whatever you like."

Shaped pancakes? "What about curious chocolate Labradors?" It seemed only right he have a dog pancake in Eliot's honor. After all, Eliot had been his first kiss in quite some time.

Mia chuckled, pouring the batter in the pan. "One chocolate lab coming right up."

Kenton glanced around his kitchen as he sat. The living room had looked… well… lived in. Messy and scattered with kid paraphernalia. But the kitchen was spotless and clutter-free. Since she worked in a bakery, that made sense, and he was grateful.

"He didn't wake you this morning, did he?" She asked as she flipped the pancake.

"*Wake* is a mild way to put it." His tone was playful.

She glanced over her shoulder at him. An embarrassed blush traced across her nose, reddening her face from cheek to cheek. "I am so sorry." The color was endearing on her. His words faltered as he stared at her.

She was lovely, and he was oh-so-pathetic for the way he ogled her over a simple flush. "It—It's fine. The kiss was a *little* on the wet side, but nothing I can't handle."

The color deepened, and her lips mashed together, holding in a laugh. "He is rather affectionate." She plated the dog pancake and added a few sausage links before handing it to him. "Butter and syrup are already on the table."

A minute later, she tossed the pan in the sink and joined him. Before beginning to eat, she cut up a sausage link into small pieces and put a few on each girl's plate.

"Do they like the same things?" he asked, unsure of what to say about the kids.

"Mostly, but they are very much individuals. I like that about them." She poured syrup over her pancake. "You met Emma last night." She indicated the twin in blue. "And this is Ava. She's the quieter one." The little girl peeked at him from under golden eyelashes.

"Hi," Kenton said, feeling uncomfortable. Kids were all new to him. As long as they never changed clothes, he'd be okay at telling them apart. "I looked up pictures of the fire," he said. "Scary."

"It was," she admitted, lowering her voice. "I was terrified, but I had to react. In the moment, I couldn't think about anything but getting them out. They're the only family I have."

"Grandparents?" Didn't she have anyone to help her?

She shook her head. "My parents passed away when I was a girl, and their father's family lives in Alaska. I video chat with them periodically so they can see their grandchildren, but my sister's will was clear. The girls are mine to raise. That's why I was so thankful for your mother's offer. Finding another place to live on short notice with two kids and a dog seemed almost impossible." She was speaking rapidly, as if she had to make her case to him.

"I'm not going to ask you to leave, you know," he said. She needed to relax, since no way was he tossing her and two little kids out on their butts. That wasn't who he was. He wouldn't do that to her.

"Thanks." She let out a sigh and flashed him another smile. It made his chest tighten. "That's very kind of you. You have no idea how much this helps."

Kenton returned her smile, and his stomach fluttered. He took a deep breath, smothering the sensation. This wasn't the time or place. "Were all your belongings destroyed?"

"I was able to salvage a few things," she said, "but most of it had so much water and smoke damage that it wasn't worth keeping. Insurance helped me replace what I needed in the short term. Cribs for the girls and clothes and the like."

Kenton watched Eliot approach Emma's high chair and swipe a piece of sausage from the tray. Not a difficult trick for a dog whose head was level with the table, but not acceptable behavior, either.

"Mia—" He tried to get her attention.

"My apartment is being redone, and the parts of the building destroyed by the fire have been torn down and are being rebuilt, but I don't know when we can return."

"Yeah, I read that in the online article, too. Uh… Mia." He pointed to where Eliot was swiping food from the other twin's tray.

"Eliot, stop that," Mia said, but her tone was amused. The dog glanced at her with soulful eyes and snagged another piece of pancake.

"He's completely untrained," Kenton declared. That needed to change, and soon. He'd make allowances for some things, but not a half-wild dog.

"Not entirely. He hasn't had an accident in the house," she said brightly. "The twins, however…"

"Huh?" What kind of accident was she talking about?

"They aren't trained, either. Toddlers are messy."

Emma was smashing the remains of her pancake into her hair. "I can see that," he commented.

"Don't worry," Mia continued. "I'll scrub down the walls and floors before we move out."

Walls? He didn't like the sound of that. Even though he hadn't lived in the house much, he'd taken care to select colors appropriate to the home's age. And he'd bought furnishings that were comfortable and classic. His mom had helped him, but he'd also engaged an interior decorator for the formal rooms. This house was going to be the setting for the perfect life he was planning for himself.

If it survived this temporary invasion.

Kenton felt his annoyance rise, which wasn't fair. Mia was in a bind. Maybe it was best to keep his distance, so at least he didn't see the destruction firsthand.

He stood up and took his plate to the dishwasher. "I've got some work to do. Do you want me to help you clean up?"

"I've got it." Mia wiped Ava's hands with a paper towel.

"Thanks for breakfast, then."

Kenton kept himself occupied in his home office for several hours sorting through personal emails that had stacked up, taking care of the few things that came by regular mail, and, frankly, worrying about a child-trafficking ringleader who was on the loose somewhere in the world.

He clicked the pen in his hand as he once again reviewed his last mission, looking for the flaw in his plan that had allowed the man to slip through the net they'd cast for him. Kenton still couldn't find the error, so he turned his attention to preparing for his future. The house was almost perfect, but he had a few home improvement projects yet to be done before he'd be ready for phase two: finding someone to share it with.

That was a tougher puzzle, but he'd solve it as he had most issues in his life—with a solid plan. He wrote down a list of places where he might meet the right sort of woman and researched dating apps with high marriage rates. A surprising number of couples met and wed from those sites. That seemed promising.

Pleased with what he'd accomplished, he opened his office door and winced. The solid oak had prevented the noise from reaching him, but no longer. He headed toward the epicenter of the cacophony: his living room. When he walked through the archway, he stopped cold.

Children's music was playing, high-pitched voices singing rhyming songs. Eliot was eating some unidentifiable food from the floor in the corner. One of the girls was sitting on the rug, face wet with tears, and the other was red-faced as if angry. Mia stood between them, almost like she was playing referee. What the hell kind of chaos was this?

He was no expert, but it looked like a nap was in order for everyone.

"Maybe you could fill me in on the schedule?" Kenton asked, pitching his voice to be heard when he really wanted to bark orders until everyone was quiet.

"Sure," Mia said, picking up the teary girl and tickling her tummy. Her action seemed to have minimal effect in terms of soothing the child. "On days that I work, I get up at four. I usually leave about a half hour later, drop the girls at day care, and head to the bakery. Since I'm primarily in the kitchen, my work is done around noon or one—unless we're really busy and I have to help at the counter. I pick up the girls on my way home, so we're all home by early afternoon, which gives me plenty of time with them."

"I meant the girls' schedules. What time do they eat, nap, that sort of thing?"

"Oh, I don't do rigid schedules for them," she responded.

"Seriously?" Kenton's eyebrows shot up. That didn't seem right to him. His childhood had been orderly and on a timetable, with his mother the keeper of the clock. He had always felt that it engendered good habits and a sense of responsibility. Hell, he even credited the way he'd been raised for making him a successful soldier.

"At day care, they have a schedule for snack, nap, and playtime," she explained, "but at home, I use the free-range parenting method."

An image of free-range chickens came to Kenton's mind, and that didn't seem like the best way to raise children. "What does that mean?"

"It's a system that fosters independence by letting kids be in charge of themselves. Within limits, of course. At this age, it means letting them decide when they're hungry, for instance. Letting kids make decisions gives them confidence. And it's proven that free-range kids are happier, play outside more, and have better social skills ultimately."

Kenton eyed the two toddlers. Neither looked happy or capable of communication. He didn't want to test the outdoors part. God only knew what would happen if he let them out in the yard.

"I want the girls to follow their own instincts," Mia continued. "They'll let me know when they need something."

"They both seem cranky," he observed. "Does that mean they're letting you know they need a nap?"

"Probably," she said with a rueful smile, "but they have to learn how to go to sleep on their own, how to soothe themselves."

It took everything in him to not declare what she said ridiculous. Who came up with this stuff? That was a good question, actually. "How do you know about this?"

"From parenting books and articles," she said. "You can look it up."

"I'll take your word for it." The last thing he wanted to spend time doing was searching parenting forums that compared kids to chickens. Still, he had to admit that he had no idea how to make a kid go to sleep. He remembered his mom declaring that it was naptime, and that was the end of the discussion.

Over the sound of the music, he heard something new: whimpering. He rapidly scanned both kids. No change with either. He focused in on Eliot, who was drooling excessively. The dog's sides began to heave, and seconds later he puked on the rug in front of the fireplace. What came up gave new meaning to the expression "Technicolor yawn." Kenton could see undigested rainbow goldfish in the pile.

Mia sucked in a breath. "I'm so sorry. I'll clean it up right away." She turned one way and then the other before thrusting the twin she'd been holding into his arms.

Before Kenton could do anything, Mia dashed from the room toward the hall closet, where he kept a carpet shampooer.

The twin he held—Ava, he guessed—was squinching up her face and looked like she was getting ready to explode. He'd had a drill sergeant once who got that same expression just before he cut loose with a torrent of orders and expletives. While he was trying to decide how to manage the pending siege of tears, he felt little hands grip the edge of his athletic shorts.

He looked down. The other twin was pulling herself up using his clothing, threatening to yank his shorts down in the process.

"This is not going to work," he said to himself.

He raised his eyes and made contact with Mia's as she returned to the room. She'd heard him. Damn.

4

"How's it going, sweetie?" Shasta moved past her in the bakery's kitchen and rapidly put loaves of bread just out of the oven on a tray.

"No worries," Mia said as she switched on the giant stand mixer to make the final batch of dough for the morning.

Shasta was a squinter. The older woman had a definite way of narrowing her eyes at anything that didn't quite make sense to her. Mia felt that look directed at her.

"You've been a little frantic this morning," Shasta said in her raspy voice.

With a sigh, Mia came to lean on the counter near Shasta. "Kenton Fitzpatrick came home two days ago, earlier than his mother expected. I'm not sure he's happy about me living in his house."

"Too bad. He's a nice man, though, right? I remember him as a kid who toed the line. His mama wouldn't raise anything but a gentleman." Shasta knew Margaret as well.

25

"He is." Mia was quick to agree. He'd said at breakfast yesterday that he wouldn't make her leave, but his declaration later that day that their arrangement wasn't going to work had left her shaken. He'd been excessively polite the rest of the day, helping her clean up the mess and then distancing himself by going outside to work in the yard. "But I'm in his house."

The bell on the bakery's door jingled. "I'll be back." Shasta hoisted the tray onto her shoulder and went through the swinging door that connected the kitchen to the counter area.

Mia evaluated the dough in the mixing bowl. It looked a little sticky. Probably the higher humidity that day. She added more flour and waited, eyeing the dough as it spun around. Better. Working in the bakery had given her an of expertise with baking she'd previously lacked. She still enjoyed experimenting, particularly at home, because it relieved stress. Just the day before, she'd made dinner rolls and cookies. Baking relaxed her and added to her repertoire. She'd been pleased with the rolls, but the cookies had only been good, not great.

Not that it mattered. They were eaten regardless. And the whole point had been to take her mind off her situation. After Kenton's reaction to the chaotic scene he witnessed in his living room, Mia was giving serious consideration to moving out.

Except she hated moving. It involved so much planning. The packing would be minimal, since she and the girls had few possessions at this point, but it would still take her several loads with her small car. And then she'd have to put in a change of address at the post office and go through the hassle of getting utilities turned on in her name. So many details. And the place she'd have to move to was so far from her job and the girls' day care. Worst of all, it would be uprooting the girls again. The poor babies had had enough disruption in their young lives.

Mia eyeballed the dough again and decided she was satisfied with its consistency. She turned it out onto the counter and began dividing it into individual pieces for loaves. When Margaret had offered her Kenton's house, it seemed like the hand of fate. She'd always been one to look at such occurrences as fortuitous. From her experience, the things that just happened often led to good. There was that time she fell into conversation with a ski instructor in a diner and ended up working at a resort in Colorado for the winter. It had been lovely. Another chance meeting had led her to the Florida Keys for a stretch as a pastry chef assistant in a major hotel.

She'd kicked around the country after dropping out of college, always considering her sister's home as a sort of base. After the twins were born, Mia had stuck closer to Caroline, since she wanted to be part of her nieces' lives, but she hadn't been stagnant. The wind still blew her around from time to time, and that had been a good thing. Like this bakery job. She'd been walking down the street in the days after Caroline and her husband's deaths and smelled the comforting scent of bread baking. Mia had pushed the door of the bakery open, thinking she'd get a treat for the twins, when she saw the Help Wanted notice for a summer baker. It had seemed like fate, and she'd applied on the spot.

"I think that's the last rush of the morning." Shasta propped the door open and leaned in the doorway so they could talk and she could keep an eye on the front. "I can help you move, sweetie, if that's what you need to do."

"I don't want to." Mia sighed.

"Everything's tougher when you have kids to consider." Shasta had four grown children and several grandchildren. "You might need to think about structuring your life a little more. It really does help."

"You mean make plans?" Mia asked.

Shasta gave her an easy smile. "It's not the end of the world to know what's coming next."

"Do plans ever really work out, though? I mean, whenever I've tried it, something has gone terribly wrong." Mia thought of her own parents, who had both been planners. Their home had been hyper-organized, including a whiteboard in the kitchen mapping out both a weekly and a daily schedule for everyone in the household. As if knowing where people should be meant they were actually there. It had worked most of the time, Mia remembered, but none of it had mattered when her parents were involved in a multicar accident on the highway. Plans hadn't saved them, nor had they saved her sister.

She blew out a breath. Two generations of her family both wiped out in accidents. No one had to tell her that life was unpredictable. She'd experienced that herself.

"They don't always work. Life gives you surprises. Some good, some bad. Take my William, for example." Shasta's youngest son had recently graduated from college with a degree in engineering. "He wasn't planned, and having another baby put a real strain on the family budget." Shasta smiled again and lowered her voice. "If you tell anyone what I'm about to say, I'll deny it, but William's my favorite. In some ways, he's the best of my kids. I love them all, but there's something about him. And you're right, he wasn't planned, and it worked out great."

"See. My point exactly," Mia said. "There's no assurance of how things will go, ever." It was as good as fact to her, but it didn't help her navigate her current situation any better. She was going to have to make a change and give Kenton back his home, because it was really his castle, like the old phrase said. The beautiful home even had a castle-like turret.

Okay, decision made, she thought, as she put the dough into bread pans to rise. She'd stop by the apartment building's office, which had been unscathed in the fire, and see if she could still get a spot in their other building. The commute was going to make her life more difficult, but it couldn't be helped. She needed to vacate Kenton's house.

"Could you take Eliot for a few months?" she asked Shasta, who lived on the outskirts of town and had property enough for a dog to run.

"Of course I can," Shasta agreed readily. "I'll take good care of him for you, if that will help."

"Thanks," Mia said. She had no intention of making big plans, but she could make little arrangements to keep going.

An hour later, Mia stopped by her apartment complex on the way to the twins' day care center. After talking to the leasing agent, she felt a little better. The renovations were going well, and her original apartment would be ready for her to move back into in a month. That wasn't so bad. In the meantime, they had a unit for her in the neighboring town. She could do one month of a longer commute, and Eliot would be happy with Shasta, she hoped.

Things were looking up, Mia told herself as she headed to pick up the girls. Jen, the care provider the girls liked the most, helped Mia get them to the car. As they each strapped in a child, Mia told Jen about her housing problems and how she almost had them resolved but lamented the longer drive.

"I can help you out with that," Jen offered.

"How? Are you going to come and babysit for me in my new apartment?" Mia joked.

"No, but I might be able to offer you a place to live that's closer. I just had a 'she shed' built in my backyard."

"A what?" Mia asked. Jen was offering her a shed to live in?

Jen smiled. "It's not quite how it sounds. It's really a small cottage. Mine is set up for crafting, so I have electricity and water. It could work for a short period, and the girls might enjoy it. It would be like living in a dollhouse. Think about it."

"I will," Mia said as she put the girls' bag in the trunk of her car. "And thanks." She gave Jen a wave and got in her car.

People were generally kind. Mia had learned that long ago, which is what had made her life as a carefree single going where the wind blew her so fun. Life as a parent was full of all sorts of worries that she'd never anticipated having, but friends and acquaintances had come through for her just the same. So the message from the universe was clear. She had options, decent ones, and either way, it was only for a few weeks.

By the time she drove the ten minutes to Kenton's house, both girls were asleep in the back seat. Also a blessing of sorts. She could slip out of the car and maybe have a talk with Kenton about moving before they woke. She hadn't apologized to him sufficiently yesterday after the dog puke incident, and she wanted to express her thanks for having lived there for the past weeks. There. She'd make a nice little speech and start packing her stuff to move out tomorrow or the next day.

She pulled into the driveway, parked near the garage, and quietly got out of the car. Kenton was working on the front porch, scraping paint from a railing that she hadn't even noticed was peeling. His shirt draped across his wide frame, hinting at every line and curve hiding underneath. And the muscles in his arms rose and fell from the work. A familiar warmth bloomed in her stomach. It was the same one she had felt that night they met. She sucked down a deep breath to cool her senses. When had scraping paint become so provocative?

"Hi," she called, getting his attention as she walked closer. "I wanted to—"

"Hey," Kenton shouted, his focus behind her and his jaw set.

Mia spun around. A man was approaching her car from the opposite side. Instinctively, she hit the lock button on the key fob. He raised something black and shiny, and she thought he was going to smash the window next to Emma, but then she heard a loud bang and froze. Was that a shot?

Oh, yes, it was. The man was holding a gun!

"Get down," Kenton ordered, sprinting past her toward the shooter. The other man eyed Kenton before taking off with Kenton on his heels.

Mia crouched and made it to the car, getting in the back seat with the girls and locking the doors again. She pulled them from their seats and onto the car's floor with her. Her heart was racing, and she experienced raw fear as she never had before.

"It's okay, babies," she tried to reassure the twins, but her voice was shaking. It was definitely not okay. Someone had just threatened her nieces.

5

———————

Whoever the guy was, he was in shape, Kenton concluded after a two-block chase that ended with the man jumping into a waiting car and taking off. Kenton got the license plate, but he doubted it would help. Likely either stolen or a rental. Crooks didn't tend to drive their own vehicles.

He jogged back to the house and found Mia hunkered down in her car. When he tapped on the window, he caught a look of panic on her face before she recognized him and opened the door. Her fear needled him in a way he couldn't quite understand.

"He's gone for now. Let me help you." While she carried one twin, he took the other. He lifted the girl and held her close to his body. "Get in the house quickly." Once inside, he put the twin on her feet where Mia could take her hand. "Stay away from the windows. Go into the living room and keep them busy on the floor."

"What happened?" Mia's ponytail was askew, and her eyes wide.

"Just do what I say," he said. "Please."

Even though he hadn't left home that day and didn't think anyone could have entered, he swept the house from the attic to the basement, looking for signs of intrusion. Finding nothing to concern him, he moved to the exterior, carefully checking the garage and yard. He found a bullet embedded in the trunk of a huge oak tree near Mia's car. The single shot must have sounded to the neighbors like a backfire, since it hadn't garnered any attention. Kenton was glad for that. He needed to think and make the right contacts, because he doubted this was a simple case of attempted robbery, carjacking, or kidnapping.

This was more serious. The assailant had looked like a professional, in Kenton's estimation, based on his clothing and the type of weapon he'd carried. The missed shot surprised Kenton, though. Unless the intention had been to frighten him. If so, message received.

When he was satisfied the house was safe for the moment, he went to Mia. She looked up at him from the living room floor with less panic in her eyes but no smile. The girls were putting pieces in a children's puzzle and seemed unaffected.

"We're safe for now," he said, wanting Mia to have that much comfort. "I need to make some calls."

"What happened? What was that man trying to do?" She kept her voice level, but it was underpinned with stress.

"I don't have all the answers yet. Just give me a little time." He went to his office and called his commanding officer first, describing what had occurred. He was told to expect a call back within the hour. Next, he talked to Anderson and Patrick to review it with them. Re-examining the incident helped Kenton comb through the details in his mind. Each time, he played the scene in slow motion again, looking for any clue he may have missed.

By the time he finished with that, his CO, Colonel Schaffer, was back on the line.

"Do you have a woman and two kids living with you?" the colonel asked immediately when Kenton picked up the call. "I thought you were single."

"I am. They're living here temporarily." Kenton explained briefly about the fire and his mother's offer for Mia and the girls to live in his house.

"Bad luck for them," Colonel Schaffer said when Kenton finished. "Intelligence has picked up a threat against you. No details, but there's some international chatter. We haven't narrowed down who it is, but they appear to know about your houseguests."

"You think the threat could be directed at them as well." Kenton didn't like the sound of that.

"It's possible. If someone wants to hurt you, getting at the kids or her would be a way of doing that," the colonel said.

"But she's not my girlfriend, and those aren't my kids. I'd never even met them before I arrived home a few days ago," Kenton argued. This was turning into a nightmare. He could handle a threat against him. It wouldn't be the first one. But including Mia and the girls…

"You can imagine how it looks," Colonel Schaffer pointed out. "Anyone might assume there's more of a connection than there is. Keep a sharp eye out, and we'll get back to you as soon as we have more info."

"Son of a bitch," Kenton muttered when he put his phone down. A series of things had become obvious to him. One: he and his house had been watched, probably starting before he'd arrived home from his recent mission. Two: he wished his mother had never offered his home to a stranger who was now potentially in danger. That led to three: he had to protect Mia and her nieces, and he would have to keep them close to do that.

That last was a complication he didn't want or need, but he felt obligated. Before going to speak to Mia, he called Patrick and Anderson back, updating them with what the colonel had said. They both agreed he needed to sit tight and keep his guests safe and offered to respond at a moment's notice if he needed them.

The statement was unnecessary, since they'd had each other's backs since elementary school, but it was good to know that help was a call away.

"The guy went for the kids first," Anderson had pointed out during the conversation. "You know what I'm thinking. It could be connected to Ocampa."

Anderson was right: he hadn't needed to spell it out. Kenton had already thought of the same thing.

He rose and went to find Mia, knowing she wasn't going to like what he had to say. No one would. When he reached the living room, it was eerily quiet. Mia sat on the couch, folding a basket of laundry. The girls were sleeping on the rug by the fireplace with an afghan over them. Even Eliot was calm for a change.

"They look peaceful," he said as his eyes swept over the room.

"They didn't see enough to be scared," Mia said, but her tone suggested that she had.

"Nothing to worry about right now. The house is secure." He wanted to give her some comfort. She looked tired and drawn, which wasn't a surprise since she'd been up since four and worked a full shift—and was caring for two toddlers. What must it have been like for her to suddenly be a parent? That and the loss of her sister must have been tough enough. And then the apartment fire. A lesser person might have crumbled, but she must be the resilient type. He hoped so, given what he was about to say.

"Good. That's good," she repeated as if trying to convince herself. "The girls and I will be out of your hair by tomorrow, or the next day at the latest, so you won't need to worry about us anymore."

"What?"

"I've got two leads on other places to stay." She matched up socks as she spoke. "I'll decide tonight and make the arrangements."

"You can't go," he said, putting it bluntly but keeping his voice gentle. "It's not safe for you."

"What do you mean?" She looked up at him, and he saw the panic return to her eyes.

He crossed the room and took a seat next to her. "The attack today wasn't just on me. I think it included you and the girls, too."

"What?" She angled her body toward his. "What are you talking about? Wasn't it some random thing?"

He shook his head, trying to figure out the best way to explain that an international criminal was watching them and might be contemplating something far worse.

She blinked rapidly, but he saw tears forming in her eyes. The glow of happiness he'd seen in her was completely gone, and he wasn't sure what he could do.

"Please try not to worry," he found himself saying. What did he mean? Of course she should be worried. "That is, I'm going to take care of this. I'm already working on—" Oh, crap. She was looking even more upset now. "I mean, anything you need, I'm going to—"

"I could do with a hug," she said, giving him a weary smile despite the tears that ran down her cheeks.

He hesitated. He wanted to comfort her, but dealing with women in distress wasn't his norm. "Sure," he said and pulled her against him. They were still sitting on the couch, but she buried her head in the crook between his shoulder and neck. He placed one arm low on her waist and the other around her shoulders and held her. A soft sound came from her, and he assumed it was a sob, but he didn't know what to say to make any of this better. So he just held her and massaged little circles across her shoulders.

When she pulled back a few minutes later, her eyes were red, but she seemed steadier as she straightened her posture and put a little distance between them. He immediately missed her softness against him. What was that about? He wasn't a hugger by nature, but she'd felt right in his arms.

"We have to stay?" She rubbed her fingers over her cheeks, removing the last traces of the tears.

He nodded. "We'll have to work out a schedule."

"We do?" She sounded instantly wary. Did she think he was trying to control her?

"I need to know when you're coming and going," he explained. "When the girls are outside playing, for instance. Everything has to be coordinated so I can provide maximum security."

"Oh, I hadn't thought about that." Some of her stress lessened. "If that's what it takes to keep them safe."

"And you, too." It was just as important to keep her out of harm's way. He'd never forgive himself if his mother's kind gesture of providing shelter for a woman in need resulted in something tragic.

"I'm an adult," she said. "I can manage myself. All that matters is the girls."

Kenton almost smiled. There was something momma-bearish about her that appealed to him. He understood that need to protect others, to keep them safe. As the captain of his SEAL team, he felt that responsibility whenever they were on missions. Maybe his role was like being a parent. He performed it through careful planning and extensive training. There wasn't time for the latter in this situation, but he could put plans in place.

He studied her for a minute. Mia had gone back to folding laundry, but he'd seen enough to recognize a soldier ready to do battle. He could work with that.

"We'll figure it out together, then." After the girls were in bed for the night, he'd pull up a spreadsheet and outline a daily schedule.

"How long will this last?" Mia asked.

Was she thinking she'd be able to move out next week or in a month when her apartment was refurbished? He had to put an end to that kind of thinking. "Until the threat is neutralized."

"Oh," she said. "I guess… that makes sense."

6

Kenton hadn't liked that the twins went to day care the following day, but he hadn't seen a better option. He *had* run a check on the facility and noted its excellent safety record and firm policies about who could pick up kids. He'd deemed it acceptable since Mia had to work. Still, when he was out running some errands, he drove by the day care twice. Each time he parked across the street for a few minutes and watched.

He'd seen nothing to worry him, but while he worked on projects around the house and kept up with communications with his CO, he considered a different option for the coming days. If he kept the twins at home with him, he could guarantee their safety. He would know where they were and what they were doing every minute. There would be no unknowns. With that in mind, he researched how to care for toddlers. He avoided the free-range parenting sites and focused on a more traditional route. After three hours of reading, he concluded that eighteen-month-olds didn't seem that complicated. Certainly nothing he couldn't handle as long as he went into it prepared.

After dinner, he helped Mia clear away the dishes while the twins lingered over cookies. He thought it a good time to inform her of his plan to watch the kids. The more he'd thought about it throughout the day, the better he felt. It eliminated a place where the kids were more vulnerable and helped her with a childcare problem she'd mentioned.

"I'll take care of them tomorrow," he declared without preamble.

"Huh? What?" Mia had been bent over the dishwasher and straightened up quickly. "Take care of the girls? Why?"

"Didn't you say you'd have to take the day off tomorrow because the day care wasn't open?" She'd mentioned this when she got home. The day care was having professional development for their staff, and Mia had forgotten about it. She needed to keep a calendar so those sorts of things didn't catch her by surprise.

"Well, yeah, but…" She looked toward Emma, who was mushing the remains of her cookie between her fingers.

"I'll watch them so you can go to work," he said. "Besides, I think they'll be safer with me."

"Have you taken care of kids before?" Her gaze was back on him.

"I've babysat some enlisted men. Does that count?" He shot her a grin to which she rolled her eyes. "I haven't, but I did some online research and downloaded a book about establishing routines with kids. I haven't read the entire thing yet, but I've skimmed most of it." It had been organized in chapters dedicated to different age groups and activities, making it easy to get through the relevant parts quickly.

"A book." She drew out the word, her tone more teasing than condescending. "Sounds like you are all set and will whip the girls into shape and out of toddlerhood in a week." She put the last of the items in the dishwasher, closed it, and pushed the start button.

"Your confidence in me is exhilarating."

Her lips thinned as she held in a laugh. "I believe that's just *your* confidence rousing you."

"Possibly." Kenton smirked, undeterred. "I've worked out a daily schedule on a spreadsheet, but I'll print out some quick-glance guides to have with me during the day." He planned to put those on card stock and place them around the house for easy access. "You might want to use them, too."

She leaned against the counter. "Your reconnaissance mission sounds like it was a great success. I look forward to seeing you in action."

He eyed her. Was she agreeing to this too easily? Her face gave nothing away. Which meant either she was being sincere, or she had one hell of a poker face.

"Okay, then," he said. "I've got kid duty."

The following morning, Kenton checked his watch. He had time to take Emma and Ava for a short walk before their morning naps. He'd seen on the refrigerator the nap, snack, and play schedule that the day care provided and decided to use it as a guide, since they were professionals. So far, he'd been right on with breakfast and morning playtime. He'd even managed to get them dressed without incident. He dressed Emma in red and Ava in yellow. He was pretty certain he knew which twin was which at this point, but he didn't want to get confused over the course of the day.

Since he didn't have a play set available, their scheduled outdoor time would have to be accomplished with a walk around the neighborhood.

"Okay, girls, time to get in the stroller," he said, filling his voice with enthusiasm.

Ava looked up from where she and her sister were playing with blocks but didn't move. Emma ignored him entirely as she snapped together two colorful, oversized pieces.

"Stroller time," he repeated. "Don't you want to go for a walk?"

Why was he asking toddlers questions? He stopped himself. He was the adult in charge, and they should do what he asked. He moved closer to them. Ava got to her feet and toddled toward him, so he picked her up.

"Leave the blocks, Emma."

"No," she said.

Kenton had heard that word often enough from her. She'd said no to a pair of socks, to cereal, and even to moving from the kitchen to the living room. She was testing him. He'd read that some toddlers did that. He hadn't overreacted, which had allowed him to accomplish his goals. She'd put socks on, although not the ones she'd said no to. She'd eaten breakfast, a different kind of cereal. He couldn't claim victory for the room change, because Ava had taken Emma's hand and led her twin to the living room.

"Don't want to," Emma said, not looking up from her play.

"That's not an option. Ava and I are going for a walk, and you're coming." He stepped closer, and the ball of his foot landed on the edge of a block. "Son of a…" Kenton bit off the rest of the phrase. He wanted to hop around the room holding his foot, but he had a child in one arm and had to be the adult in the room.

Emma's attention was still focused on the blocks. Jesus, she was stubborn, and he was getting irritated. What had the book suggested he do in this situation? He thought back to the chapter on toddler behavior but couldn't remember what it said.

"Okay, you in the stroller first," he said to Ava, making up his mind. He went to the entryway and strapped her in. Before going back for Emma, he checked the bag with water bottles and snacks he'd put in the basket under the stroller earlier. Being prepared and organized were keys to being successful with little kids. With anything, he thought.

As he turned to go back into the living room, he felt little hands on his leg. Emma was using him as a ladder to climb into the stroller.

"Glad you could join us," he said as he did the buckle on the strap. He wanted to gloat, since he'd won in a way, but that would be childish. Plus, he had to admit that he had no idea what he'd been going to do in the living room to make her comply.

Before opening the front door, he took a minute to scan the street. Nothing seemed out of place, so he pushed the stroller through and started on a course through the neighborhood that he'd already mapped out in his head. He might have to cut it short, since getting the kids into the stroller had taken longer than he'd expected.

After ten minutes of walking, he pulled up in the shade of an oak tree and reached for the twins' water bottles. It was a cool day, but hydration was important. He handed one to Emma, but she batted it out of his hand.

"No," she said as the bottle rolled across the sidewalk. Her little jaw stuck out, letting him know she was displeased.

"Mine," Ava said softly.

"Yours?" Kenton retrieved the bottle that had rainbow stripes going around it. "This one is yours?"

Ava reached for it, giving him a shy smile. He stroked a hand over her hair. This one was a sweetheart. Emma had her good qualities, too, but the twins were night and day.

"So I take it this belongs to you?" He held out the bottle with stars on it to Emma, who immediately took it. "I didn't know there were so many rules," he muttered to himself. "How about a snack?" He pulled out two small bags of crackers he'd found in the kitchen.

"Don't like those," Emma said. When he glanced at Ava, she was quietly shaking her head.

Why were they in the cabinet if neither of the girls would eat them? Well, that's probably why they were there and not in the basket of snacks on the counter. He blew out a breath. He should have realized that.

"Let's go home," he said half to himself and began pushing the stroller again.

When they were halfway there, a bee buzzed close to Ava. She squealed and swatted at it, bumping Emma in the head with her hand. Ten seconds later they were both crying, and Kenton had no idea why. The bee had flown off, and Emma couldn't be hurt.

"Hey, it's okay," he said, trying to soothe them. "Nothing's wrong." But they both continued to cry, and despite his efforts to locate the problem, they kept it up until falling asleep just before they reached home.

Usually, when he approached his house, it was with a sense of pride in the knowledge that he owned the beautiful property. That day, he was filled with relief. It was a beautiful, crisp autumn day, but he felt nothing but frustration at the circumstances he found himself in. He wasn't meant to be the guardian of kids who weren't his.

This was way outside the plan he had for himself. He was supposed to be searching for a woman to share his home with, and then he'd think about kids of his own. He couldn't do any of that until the threat against him, Mia, and the twins was eliminated.

As he pushed the stroller up to the front porch, Mia's car turned into the driveway. She was early, way early. He watched as she stepped from the car. Part of him was worried that something had happened to bring her home before her shift was done, and part of him was enjoying watching her.

She was beautiful. His assessment of that hadn't changed since the night when he'd discovered her living in his house. She was caring and nice, but definitely not a pushover. His mind went back to those few minutes when he'd held her two nights ago. It had been only a hug, but the feel of her body seemed to linger.

"Are they sleeping?" she asked softly as she walked across the leaf-strewn lawn to him.

"Just fell asleep. I'm going to move them to their cribs. Why are you home early?"

"I woke up at three, gulped down some coffee, and went in to get a jump on the day's baking."

Had she done that intentionally so she got home to oversee what he was doing? Didn't she trust him?

"How long have they been asleep?" she asked, gently taking the water bottle from Ava's hand.

"Five minutes." His answer was terser than he meant it to be.

"They look comfortable." She glanced at them where they sat in the shade. "Let's leave them. It's beautiful today, and we can sit on the porch while they snooze." She gestured to the porch swing he'd hung the day before.

"No. I want them to always sleep in their beds. The routine is impor-tant, even if they did go to sleep a little earlier than I had scheduled." Twenty minutes wasn't huge, but he'd have to make adjustments to accommodate the change. "I'll carry them upstairs."

"Do you need some help?" she offered.

"No, I've got this." He could carry a twin in each arm and come back for the stroller once they were settled.

"Okay, I'm going to grab a shower then." She went past him to the door, and he thought he saw a smile on her face, but it was gone in an instant.

An hour later, he had to admit that Mia had been right. Ava woke as he put her down in her crib. She might have gone back to sleep, but her movements had roused Emma—who was willing to stay in her bed but sang loudly to a stuffed rabbit. Pretty soon, both girls were singing and talking, and any chance of a nap was gone.

After giving up on that, he fed them lunch without incident other than some cheese in Emma's hair. Then he moved onto the educational part of the day. He'd read about making learning look like fun and wanted to try it. But then the girls didn't want to color inside the shapes he'd printed out for them. Both of them scribbled across the pages with no regard to the circles and squares.

The same was true of the counting and color identification lesson he tried with blocks. Neither girl could stay interested in organizing the blue blocks into piles of three or the red in piles of four for more than a few minutes. Or if one was willing to play along, the other was off running in a different direction. He'd scooped up Ava just before she stuck her little finger into an electrical outlet, and he mentally put childproofing items on a shopping list.

In the meantime, Emma developed a fascination with turning a lamp on and off by using the switch on the cord.

By the time the twins were in bed for the night, Kenton plopped onto the couch in exhaustion. How was it that he could lead SEAL missions in which he slept little and moved constantly and not be tired, but keeping track of two little girls had done him in.

Mia came in from the kitchen with a beer in her hand. "Here. You earned this."

"Thanks," he said, accepting the drink. Mia had stuck around throughout the afternoon and early evening, but she'd let him handle the girls. He'd almost asked for help, but there was no good reason he couldn't manage it. At least, that's what he'd insisted to himself.

Mia sat down next to him, smiling. "Do you see why I parent differently? Trying to maintain a rigid schedule just frustrates everyone. Letting the girls do what is natural to them is better for them and you."

"They run you ragged, too," he said. He'd seen that with his own eyes. She had to give, give, give.

"Maybe, but I'm not fighting their natures."

"I think they'll follow a routine if I enforce it for a few days." He took a swallow of his beer.

She shook her head. "You can't predict toddlers. They play when they want, and they sleep and eat when they need to. It's simple."

To Kenton, following that approach felt like giving in, which was something he wasn't good at. The book he'd read insisted that a scheduled child became a well-organized and successful adult. And wasn't that the goal of child-rearing?

"I'm going to keep trying," he said, knowing he sounded stubborn.

"I'm home tomorrow," she said, "so you're free to work on other things."

"No, I'll help care for them." It came out as more of a command than he intended, but it was important to him. He did have several projects he wanted to accomplish during his leave, but they could wait.

"So you can prove a point?" Her eyebrow arched up.

"I think it's the right thing to do." The amused expression on her face disappeared at his words. Did she think he was being critical of how she'd raised the kids so far? He was on the verge of apologizing for that when she stood up.

"All right. I'm heading to bed." She left the room before he could say anything else.

Kenton listened as she went up the stairs. Before going to the guest room she was using, she paused outside the room the twins were in, and the door quietly opened and closed. After a minute, her soft footsteps continued down the hall. She was good with the kids, but it seemed to him that things could be better, be easier for her.

He reached for one of the quick-glance guides sitting on the coffee table and studied it. He'd need to make some revisions based on what he'd learned that day. He pulled a pen from his pocket and got to work.

7

———————

"What's this?" Mia asked, peering at the legal-size piece of paper hanging on the refrigerator door. Since she had the day off, she'd slept late, which was unusual for her but was probably due to worrying half the night about the handsome near-stranger whose house she was inhabiting and who had very definite ideas about things. She'd woken with a start and dashed down the hall to find the girls were already up and out of their cribs. After grabbing a robe, she'd gone to the kitchen to see what was happening.

"The improved schedule," Kenton said. He was wiping down counters while the twins ate. Both girls seemed surprisingly content. She knew from experience that never lasted long.

"Really?" she whispered as her brain absorbed the incredible detail. Every minute of the day appeared to be planned—and not just for the girls. For her, Kenton, and even Eliot. What kind of nonsense was this? She'd been willing to play along to a point, but this was ridiculous. "What if I don't need a bathroom break at one?"

"I thought you might like that after lunch," he said, a look of concern on his face.

"I see." Mia kept looking through the schedule all the way until bedtime. At least the portion of the evening left after the girls were down was untouched, except for Eliot's final walk of the day. Mia was tempted to pencil something in. Something a little outrageous. Kissing on the sofa or wine on the moonlit back deck. What would Mr. By-the-Book do then?

She had enjoyed his hug the other day, even if she'd shocked him by asking for it. After a brief hesitation, he'd taken her in his arms, and it had been the safest she'd felt in months. Which was an odd thought, since she usually never felt unsafe—even after her sister's death when she'd become an instant parent, or even in the wake of the apartment fire.

But she wasn't going to trade her freedom to choose how she went through her day for safety.

"Maybe we should start small," she suggested. "We could just use the same nap schedule as the day care, for instance."

"Not enough," he said. "We need routine in everything we do."

"Including Eliot." She pointed to the three times a day when he got his walks.

"Yep, he needs to be taken out on a schedule."

"Why? He may be a little untrained," she said, ignoring the side-eyed look he shot her, "but he's never had an accident in the house. And I do take him out morning, afternoon, and evening, just not at precisely the same time every day. I don't see why that matters."

"It does," Kenton insisted. "And it's the way I like things."

Mia bit back her retort, reminding herself that she and her nieces were guests in his home. His mother had been generous to her, and he hadn't tossed her out when he'd arrived back from his deployment. However, she was stuck there because of something in his world, something she had nothing to do with and no control over. Being homeless and in danger was a double whammy, but it left her in no position to argue.

"Fine. We'll follow your schedule today," she conceded, "and tomorrow they can go back to day care."

"Nope, that's not happening," he said before she even finished speaking.

"But that *is* their routine, and I thought routine was all-important," she argued. The girls were hers in every sense of the word. Being dictated to about their care was getting on her nerves. His need to schedule and desire to have control might have seemed a bit of a lark to her at first. What the heck? She could use a little break from being a single mom, but she wasn't giving total control over to him.

"They'll be safer here with me." He returned the cleaner he'd been using on the counters to an upper cabinet.

"The day care has an excellent safety rating… Oh, that's not what you meant," she said, her annoyance dissipating slightly. He was referring to the danger hanging over them. "Wouldn't it be better to have them out of the house?"

He crossed his arms over his chest. His stance was wide, a warrior ready to do battle. "I can't guarantee their safety unless I'm with them. I wish you weren't working, either, but I don't suppose you'd consider quitting."

"Of course not," she said. She wouldn't quit the bakery even if she were financially able to. The type of work and the people there appealed to her more than any other job she'd had.

"That's what I figured," he said, "but you've got to let me do my best by the girls."

She huffed out a sigh. He had their best interests at heart, and she didn't mean to be difficult, but this was a mess, a damn mess. The situation was complicated, to say the least. But it wouldn't last forever. Her apartment would be ready to live in soon enough, and her life would be hers again, provided the threat was taken care of.

"Are you sure you can do it?" she asked, not meaning to insult him, but he'd had a tough time of it the day before. Still, she'd never felt that she needed to interfere for the girls' safety. She'd been close to doing so when Emma developed a fascination for the outlets that she'd never had before, but Kenton had handled that. His care had been competent, and, she reasoned, he was a highly trained military officer. That had to mean something.

"I managed yesterday," he said, sounding confident. "Today will be better."

She nodded her approval, since she was unable to come up with an objection that she thought might work. The girls would be fine, and Kenton would figure out that time management skills were lost on toddlers. No one would be hurt as a result.

Early the next morning, Mia had to admit that Kenton's offer to watch the girls made it easier to get to work on time. She'd never relished bundling her nieces into the car during the predawn hours and dropping them off at day care before she'd had coffee. Going straight to the bakery saved her time and trouble, so she couldn't complain. And after watching Kenton with the twins the day before, she felt assured that all would be well. He'd had a few difficulties, mostly battles of will with Emma, but he'd prevailed.

And he was resourceful. Before noon, a man he had introduced as Anderson dropped off childproofing supplies, including outlet covers and latches for the cabinet doors. Mia had played with the girls while Kenton spoke with his friend on the porch. The snatches of conversation she'd overheard suggested that Anderson was a fellow SEAL and knew about the threats against them. When Kenton came back inside, he had efficiently gone to work installing the items.

Mia drained her third cup of coffee of the morning and surveyed her accomplishments. In addition to the bakery's usual offerings, she had made loaves of cinnamon bread, blueberry pound cakes, and petits fours coated in pink icing. When she first accepted the job, she'd worried that she'd become bored with it. She'd always worked the front of the house, talking to and serving customers. She'd even felt it was her special talent, since she was good at making conversation and getting guests to feel welcome.

During the months that she'd worked in the kitchen, she'd found it rewarding in a different way. Much of the work was repetitive. She made the same recipe for cake doughnuts every day, after all. At times, though, she'd welcomed that familiarity, as her life had been chaotic in other ways. With her sister's death and the twins becoming hers, she'd needed the steadiness and the solitude of the kitchen.

But there were opportunities for creativity, for trying something new as well. Like today. She smiled to herself as she dusted flour on her hands before punching down dough.

"You're a whirlwind today," Shasta said, coming through the swinging door. "Those blueberry pound cakes are practically running out the door. There's only one left."

"Really?" She'd made two dozen.

"Yes, ma'am. Gotta go." The jingle of the front door sent Shasta back out of the kitchen.

Mia finished punching the dough and checked on the cookies she had in the oven. They were just starting to crisp around the edges. Two more minutes would do it.

"Hi, sweetie." Margaret Fitzpatrick popped her head in the back door. "Something smells divine. I can usually resist, but…" Margaret's clothing boutique was next door, and it wasn't unusual to see the older woman in the kitchen.

"Come have a seat." Mia gestured to a stool tucked under the counter. "The cookies are just about out."

"How's my son?" Margaret asked when Mia handed her a still-warm cookie on a plate.

"Good." Handsome and single, doing her head in in more ways than one. "He's watching the girls for me."

"He is?" Margaret's eyes went wide.

It suddenly occurred to Mia that Kenton might not want his mother to know about the threat against them. "There was a problem with the day care, so he's stepping in for the day."

"That'll be good for him," Margaret said, biting into her cookie. "Keep him busy and out of trouble. How are the girls?"

"They're doing fine. Emma's still a pistol. I do wonder if part of her behavior is connected to her parents' deaths. She seems to want to act out, and Ava withdraws."

"What were their personalities before?" Margaret asked as she finished her cookie.

"Emma's always been the leader of the two." She'd been born first and was definitely dominant. "I think those qualities just got magnified." She'd read articles about helping toddlers grieve and tried to follow their advice.

"Give them time and lots of love," Margaret suggested. "They've had so much upheaval."

"That's what I'm trying to do," Mia said, appreciating Margaret's words of wisdom. She clearly knew something about raising successful children.

"These cookies are delicious." Margaret picked up the last crumb on her plate.

"It's a new recipe that I've been playing with." It was the same basic recipe Mia had made at home a few days earlier, but she'd made some subtle adjustments, and she was pleased with the outcome.

"It's a winner." Margaret stood and pushed the stool back under the counter. "Would you save me a few, and I'll take them home to my husband?"

"Of course." Mia hadn't met Kenton's father, and she wondered about him. Did he have the same broad shoulders and square jaw as his son? What was his personality like? Mia recognized some of Kenton's traits in his mother. She, too, was organized and dedicated—but warm and friendly at the same time. Kenton showed the first traits clearly, and, Mia supposed, since he hadn't kicked her out of his house, he must have more of his mother in him than she initially realized.

He was good to her. He'd been kind to her and the girls. They just had different approaches to how to live.

After Margaret went out the back door with a promise to drop back by later for the cookies, Mia finished the day's baking and cleaned the kitchen. She was measuring ingredients into sealable containers for the next day's first batch of dough when Shasta returned.

"I closed up the store ten minutes early. The cases are empty, and I feel like I've been run ragged," Shasta declared with a dramatic sigh.

"Maybe you need some help out there." Mia moved on to the next ingredient.

The older woman smiled. "You know I complain, but I love every minute of it." Mia laughed, because she did know that about her coworker. "I love things to be a little hectic. Makes me feel alive."

Mia felt the truth of that statement. Maybe that's why she resisted the idea of a schedule so much. "Good thing you don't live where I do. Kenton has established a routine so rigid that bathroom breaks are built in."

"Good lord." Shasta squinted up her eyes in a familiar gesture. "That boy was always regimented, maybe even a bit stiff in his interactions. That was true when he was a little one, and I used to babysit him."

Mia snapped a plastic lid on a flour container. "I wouldn't say he's stiff, exactly. He's trying to be helpful with the girls, and I sure do appreciate that. I think being in control and trying to manage everything is just his way."

"How's that working with toddlers?" Shasta grabbed the mop bucket from the utility room and rolled it toward the door to the front.

"There's a learning curve," Mia admitted with a small grin, remembering how Emma had refused to eat her peas at dinner the night before. Mia would have either let it go or cajoled the girl into trying at least one, but Kenton had sat there, patiently insistent, until Emma had given in, eaten the peas, and even declared that she liked them. "But he appears to be working it out."

"Good for him," Shasta said and left the kitchen, leaving Mia to think about her housemate.

He was different from anyone she'd ever known—and certainly unlike any man she'd dated. Those guys were always the casual types. They didn't take themselves seriously. She'd had a lot of fun with them, and that's all she'd been looking for.

Kenton was a different kind of man altogether. And there was something appealing about him that she hadn't expected. It wasn't only his
killer looks and what she suspected was an amazing body under his
clothes. It was something else, a desire to make things perfect when
nothing ever could be, that she found endearing.

8

"**D**own, Eliot!" Kenton commanded when Mia came through the door after work and the overexcited dog launched himself at her. Kenton was used to others, even dogs, obeying when he gave an order, but Eliot had his paws on Mia's shoulders and was trying to lick her face.

"I'm happy to see you, too," Mia said to the dog, taking his front paws from her blouse and returning them to the floor. She dropped to one knee next to Eliot and stroked his ears until the dog rolled onto his back with a sigh.

"He needs some actual training," Kenton said. "He can't be jumping like that."

"No harm done, and he doesn't jump on the girls. He's very protective of them, as a matter of fact."

"I guess that explains his reaction to the delivery guy today. The girls were playing on the front porch, and I thought Eliot was sleeping. He wasn't. Poor guy got one foot on the step, and Eliot hit him square in the chest. I didn't think that dog could move that fast."

"Was he knocked down?" Mia's face was full of concern.

"Flat on his back. I helped him up, and he seemed fine. He did say that he was marking the house as having a dangerous dog in the company's system so other drivers wouldn't get flattened." Kenton felt a little bad about that.

"You'll get a reputation," Mia said to Eliot. "I suppose some basic training might be a good thing. Maybe obedience school isn't such a bad idea."

Kenton considered offering to train the animal. He'd worked with canine units in the military and had an affinity for the job. He even thought that, when he retired from the SEALs, dog training for the police or military might be his next career. Eliot could be a good test subject. Kenton figured if he got the recalcitrant animal under control, he could train any dog. But he was hesitant to link Mia's life to his any more than it already was. They were together out of necessity, not choice—and he didn't know about her, but he had other plans for himself.

Mia rose, cocking her head to one side. "Where are the girls?"

"Asleep in their cribs." He was proud about that one. The twins didn't fight sleeping in their beds at night, but daytime was a different thing. He'd put them down still awake, and after ten minutes of chattering with each other, they'd gone to sleep.

"At naptime?" she said, delight in her eyes.

Before he could respond, she wrapped her arms around his neck and snugged her body against his in a hug, bouncing up and down in excitement. He put his hands on her waist to steady her, but the friction created between them had his mind going places it shouldn't. He'd tried not to notice the fullness of her breasts, making a conscious effort to keep his eyes on her face when they spoke. But when she was up against him, he couldn't miss the lushness of her curves. What would it be like…

He eased her back reluctantly. "Glad you're happy about it."

"I am. How was the rest of the day?" She wasn't hugging him anymore, but she was close enough that he could see the dusting of freckles across her nose and cheeks. And her scent was intoxicating. He'd noticed that she wore a floral perfume, but after a day at the bakery, she smelled of sugar and spice.

"Not bad," he said. Things had gone fairly smoothly. The girls played according to the schedule, including working on their numbers and colors as he'd wanted them to. He'd had to cut the outside play short after Eliot's episode with the delivery driver, but he had to admit to being pleased that Mia seemed interested in his successes. She hadn't agreed with him about scheduling the day, but she was willing to let him try. "The morning snack was an issue. Can you leave me a list of what each of them likes?"

Mia smiled at him. This close was like a jolt to the heart. "I can, but it changes without warning. I find that offering them three choices works. They can each pick one snack."

"Okay, that makes sense," he said, tucking that information away. "How was your day?"

"Busy, but good. I saw your mom." Mia removed her shoulder bag and hung it on a peg near the front door. "She took some cookies home for your father."

"He'll like that." Kenton laughed. "He has a sweet tooth." His dad was tall and lean, but he loved candy, cookies, and sweets of all varieties. Kenton did, too, but he rarely indulged.

"I should get a shower while they're still sleeping," Mia said. "It's a rare treat."

He wanted to object to her showering, since he hated the thought of the spicy scent disappearing from her skin, but she had flour on her shirt and probably was happy to have a few minutes to herself.

"Yeah," he agreed. "I should check in with my CO and team while I have the chance."

Her face turned serious and her shoulders stiffened, and he regretted reminding her of the danger they were in. She shouldn't have to deal with any of this. It was just bad luck on her part that she was in his home and linked to him. It seemed that she'd had a run of bad luck.

"Any developments?" she asked.

"Not that I know of," he said, "but maybe they'll have news for us." He reached for her, touching her arm but resisting the temptation to pull her into another hug. "I'm doing everything I can to keep you and the girls safe. I hope you believe that."

"I do." Her smile was tentative now. "And I appreciate that. Glad to have one of the good guys on my side." She went past him and up the stairs, leaving him wishing he could have done something to reassure her. If he knew where the threat originated, he could respond more effectively.

It was the not knowing that got to him. Maybe today, he thought as he headed for his office, he'd get some answers. He checked his email and saw an invitation from his CO to a secure video call in ten minutes. He went ahead and connected to it and found Anderson and Patrick already in the meeting.

"Hey, man, good to see you," Anderson said. "Did you get the child-proofing done?"

"Yeah, it didn't take long." He'd had the job completed within an hour. The girls were guests in his home, but they deserved to be safe. And, he reasoned, he would have kids of his own in the house someday. It would be one thing that wouldn't have to be done at that time.

"You had to childproof your perfect house?" Patrick said with a smile.

"Do all kids try to stick their fingers in outlets?" Kenton avoided answering the question by posing one of his own.

"I think it's universal," Anderson said. "That's why they make the covers."

"Point taken," Kenton responded.

"How are you managing with the insta-family?" Patrick asked. He had been a father longer than Anderson, with a daughter going into third grade, so he saw things from a different angle.

"It's not like that," Kenton was quick to say. "They aren't my family. But I have learned that there's no downtime with kids. I'm behind on my home improvement projects and the other things I'd hoped to accomplish while on leave." Earlier in the day, he'd taken the girls onto the front porch with him, thinking that he'd be able to replace some boards while they played. He'd managed to remove two pieces of rotten wood, but that had been the end of it.

"Kids upset any schedule you put in place," Anderson said. Discovering he was a dad a year or so ago had definitely changed his life. Now he was married, with a second baby on the way.

Kenton considered telling his buddies about the routines he was trying to establish but stopped himself. He'd wait until he could claim success with those things before saying anything. Today he'd had some triumphs, but he wasn't ready to declare victory.

"Any chance we'll meet Mia and the twins?" Patrick asked. "We'd like to."

Did Kenton want to introduce his friends and their families to his temporary houseguests? He wasn't sure. They weren't his family, even if he was watching out for them. He'd had a moment, though, when Mia had walked through his front door a few minutes ago, that had seemed right, like she belonged. And for as much as he complained about the unruly dog, he'd been damned glad when Eliot had scared the delivery driver into next week. Knowing the animal would protect the kids made Kenton feel better.

"Maybe," he said and was saved from adding to that when Colonel Schaffer and two other officers joined the call. After quick greetings, they got down to business.

"We're still digging," Colonel Schaffer explained, "but our best bet at the moment is the resurgence of a drug syndicate operating about fifty miles to your west. When you disrupted their pipeline on your South America mission last year, the syndicate all but disappeared. Now we have credible intel that they are back in business."

Kenton thought about that mission. They'd spent weeks crawling through the jungle, gathering data until they were ready to strike the central command of the drug syndicate. At the time, his team had thought they had cut the head off the hydra, but maybe they hadn't.

"And attacking SEALs personally?" Anderson asked. It happened, but it sure wasn't common.

"Our hypothesis is that they're trying to establish a safe perimeter. Fitzpatrick was the lead on that mission. If they found out he was in their neighborhood, it seems likely they would strike. It's an intimidation game. We've got the state police and the DEA watching them."

"Pardon me, sir, but the thwarted attack on Fitzpatrick's guests seems out of character for a drug cartel." Anderson, the analyst of the bunch, was always willing to question assumptions. "Those guys usually take out their enemy directly. They don't go after kids."

"What are you thinking?" Colonel Shaffer asked.

"Just this: Our last mission wasn't the success it should have been. The head of the child-trafficking ring got away from us, and he's still out there. An attack on the twin girls living in Fitzpatrick's house seems more his style. Harming the family, particularly the children, of those who have wronged him is kind of his calling card."

"We've thought of that, but our sources in northern Africa believe they have his location pinpointed. We have a team moving in on him, so he's got other problems. Besides, he has plenty of enemies. Fitzpatrick would be low on his list for retribution."

"The data on him shows that he's a spiteful bastard, if you'll pardon my language," Anderson persisted. "I wouldn't put anything past him."

"We'll take that under advisement," the colonel said. "In the meantime…"

Kenton listened as his CO assigned specific tasks to Patrick, Anderson, and the other two officers on the call.

"What's my assignment, sir?" Kenton asked. His CO couldn't expect him to twiddle his thumbs.

"Keep yourself and the people in your house safe. I don't want anything to distract you from that. Civilians don't die because of our missions. Am I making myself clear?"

"Yes, sir," Kenton said since he had no choice but to agree. He didn't like not being more involved, though.

"If you notice anything out of the ordinary, contact the team immediately. We're counting on you to protect what's yours."

He wanted to argue that Mia and the girls were not his. He had no connection to them… but he did feel an obligation. Nothing could happen to them on his watch. They'd had enough trauma in their lives without him and his problems adding to it.

"We'll talk again in forty-eight hours, unless someone has something specific to report sooner." With that, everyone signed off.

Kenton put down the pen that he'd held during the conversation. He hadn't taken notes, but he had clicked the pen several times, almost without realizing it. One of his few nervous habits. A harmless one, even if it annoyed others.

He let the conversation play back through his head, especially Anderson's objections to the idea of the drug syndicate as the perpetrator. While he thought, he organized the surface of his desk, carefully aligning the writing pad and the tray that held paper clips and such. His space was tidy, but his mind wasn't.

He was getting nowhere sitting there, though. As he stood, he heard one of the twins cry. Duty called. It was a different kind of duty, but one that tugged at him nevertheless.

9

———————

Kenton didn't like the feel of the air. All day, dark clouds had threatened, and the wind had steadily increased. Maybe the change in weather is what had the twins so cranky. Any progress he'd felt he'd made the day before had disappeared. Even Ava, who was usually a sweetheart, wouldn't cooperate on basic things like putting on her shoes when they took Eliot out in the backyard. Kenton had finally given up and let the girls go barefoot on the deck while he chucked a ball for Eliot to chase. Apparently, the dog knew how to do one thing. He could play fetch with the best of them.

Afternoon naps were the only part of the day that went well. The kids were out when Mia arrived home from work, giving both adults a little free time. Mia looked relieved when she got in the front door. With a smile that nearly knocked him backward, she went up the stairs, and he heard the shower running a few minutes later.

A gust of wind hit the house as they finished dinner, bringing with it the first of the rain. He dashed around the house closing windows against the cool, damp air brought by the storm. He was in the twins' room when thunder shook the house and lightning flashed outside. A high-pitched squeal from below had him sprinting back to the kitchen.

Mia had both girls out of their high chairs and was hugging them to her as she knelt on the floor.

"Everybody okay?" he asked, coming to a stop.

"Just scared. That was close." Just as she finished speaking, another bolt of lightning hit nearby, and the power went out.

"Shit." His curse was covered by more shrieking from the girls. He reached for Ava, taking her in his arms before helping Mia to her feet while Emma clung to her. "Let's go in the living room."

He led the way, getting them settled on the rug in front of the fireplace where the girls often played. When the girls had calmed down enough for Mia to move off a few feet, he took her arm to speak to her.

"This is a problem," he said in a low voice, not bothering to sugarcoat it. "The security system is down, which makes us vulnerable. I'm going to check the perimeter, but I need you to be on alert, too." He hadn't spoken much about his security system, but he had quietly upgraded it, adding additional cameras the day after the attack. He didn't like the idea of it going dark.

"Someone would have to be desperate to go out in this." Mia gestured toward the window, where the rain pelted and the trees swayed in the last light of the evening.

"Maybe," he said. To him, it seemed like the perfect opportunity for a home invasion. Any unusual sounds would be attributed to the storm. And with no security system alerting him to forced entry, they were sitting ducks.

A whine made him turn around. Eliot was slinking out from under a chair, inching his way closer to the twins.

"Thunder is tough on animals," Mia said before turning to address the dog. "It's okay, boy."

"I'll be back to check on all of you soon. Keep your phone on you, with my number pulled up." He waited while she did what he asked before leaving the room.

He went through the house first, checking the windows on the lower floor and all points of entry. Next, shrugging into a raincoat, he ducked his head and went out into the storm. With the rain hitting his face, his vision was limited, but he'd dealt with extreme conditions before and kept moving until he'd circled the house twice and checked the garage.

Nothing was out of place except for the branches downed by the storm. He took a minute to squint into the rain and dark. The nearby houses were all dark except for the glow of candles and lanterns. No one appeared to be moving about. He felt some of his worry ebb. He wasn't going to let his guard down, but he didn't see any reason to stand in the rain, either.

He re-entered the house through the kitchen, removing his drenched coat. It had provided some protection, but his clothes were still wet and sticking to him. At the bottom of the stairs, he paused, listening for Mia and the girls. From the living room, he heard happy voices singing a children's song. Taking that as a good sign, he went to his room and changed into dry clothes. He glanced at the small gun safe in the bottom of the closet. With the kids in the house, he didn't want to have a weapon out, but did the situation justify it?

He decided against it. There were plenty of ways he could defend his household without a gun if need be. When he returned to the living room, he found that Mia had a fire going in the fireplace and had lit candles that stood on the mantel, giving the room a homey feel.

"Glad you're back." She looked up at him. "Everything okay?"

"Seems to be." Since the girls were listening to what they said, he kept his response short and reassuring.

"Can you keep track of them for a minute? I want to get the marshmallows, chocolate, and graham crackers from the kitchen."

"S'mores," Emma shouted. Both girls looked pleased at the unexpected treat.

"Good idea," he said, plopping down on the rug between the girls. "You might need this." He pulled a flashlight from his back pocket and handed it to Mia.

"Be right back," Mia said.

He put an arm around each girl when thunder rumbled outside. The storm was moving off, but he'd checked the radar and saw another wasn't far behind it. Mia's idea to have s'mores by the fire was a great distraction.

"Here we are." Mia returned with a basket of items and spread them out near the fire. "Who wants to roast a marshmallow first?"

Kenton felt a brief moment of panic. She wasn't going to let the girls closer to the fire than they already were, was she? Mia scooted nearer to it and trapped Emma between her legs. He got her plan now, so he did the same with Ava. Eliot took up a position between them as they extended long sticks toward the fire. Mia assembled the s'mores when the marshmallows were golden brown, letting each girl put the top cracker on her own treat.

"I remember a night like this when I was young," Mia began. "Your mom and I were staying at my grandparents' house out in the country, and it had rained all day. There were puddles big enough to swim in. Just after sunset, my grandma let Caroline and me out of the house, and we ran like jackrabbits, stomping through puddles and shaking the water off plants."

Kenton wasn't sure if the girls were interested in Mia's story about running free or if it was the way she modulated her voice, but they were riveted. So much so that Mia told other stories from her childhood that involved her and the girls' mother having fun.

"Your turn." Mia smiled at him as she concluded a tale of how a boy dared her to not only touch a frog but carry it around for an entire day.

"Me?" She wanted him to tell a story? Like the kids and Eliot, he'd been happy to listen to her.

"Sure. I'll bet you've got some fascinating stories." She smiled encouragement. "You grew up in town, right?"

"I did," he said, giving Eliot, who had come to lie next to him, another rub on the belly.

"Storytelling helps to put everyone at ease." Her gaze took in Eliot. The quirk of her lips showed she was amused by his role as dog whisperer. The animal had paced nervously until finally settling against Kenton. He felt anything but ease about being put on the spot for a story. Some of his fellow SEALs were storytellers, spinning yarns of their adventures as youths. He'd never taken part in those conversations, preferring to listen. He was going to have to come up with something, though. And quick. He cast around in his memory.

"I went to Boy Scout camp every summer for several years," he began. He'd loved those weeks. Patrick was always there, and Anderson had come just the one year, but they'd made some memories that time. "One time, I wanted to stay up late to watch the Perseid meteor shower." He caught Mia's raised eyebrows and realized he'd lost his audience. Time to correct course. "It's when there are a whole bunch of falling stars on the same night." Ava's eyes grew wide with excitement. "Two buddies and I crept out of our cabin, climbed a big hill, and spent the entire night up there. We saw so many falling stars that we lost count. It was awesome, but we got caught coming back in early the next morning and had to wash the breakfast dishes for the rest of the week."

"Was it worth it?" Mia asked, her expression relaxed and happy.

"Every dish and spoon," he said. Not only had he seen dozens of meteors, he'd spent time with two of his closest friends.

"Nice story." He felt gratified at the compliment. It hadn't been as good as the ones she'd told, but he'd liked the dreamy expression on the girls' faces while he'd spoken.

"Time for bed, you two," Mia said, tapping first one girl and then the other on the nose.

Kenton had to stop himself from begging for one more story from her. The evening, despite his earlier worries about security, had been nice. There was something special about sitting in the glow of the fire.

But then he saw Emma yawn and knew the night was over. He checked his watch. It was already past their usual bedtime, and everything he'd read about raising kids had agreed that a regular bedtime needed to be observed. He rose, lifting Ava with him.

"I'll get them settled, if you want to…" Mia tilted her head toward the front door.

"Sounds like a plan," he said, surprised that he hadn't been the one to realize it was time for another security sweep.

He wished the girls good night before Mia took them upstairs by the light of a flashlight. Once alone, he moved through the house in the same pattern he had earlier, taking extra time outside now that the rain had lessened. The air was cold and clammy, but the threat of storms had moved off. A truck from the electric company turned onto the street. A good sign that the power would be restored soon. He'd stay awake until it was to make sure the security system came back up as it should.

When he returned to the living room, he found Mia cleaning up the s'more makings. She was packing up the evening, and he had a desire to prolong it.

"A glass of red wine would go well with the chocolate, if you're game," he said as his nerves flared to life, preparing for the inevitable sting should she reject his offer.

"A glass of wine?" She straightened, her voice rife with surprise. "With me?"

"Well, Eliot too. He has woken me up several days in a row now. So, I guess you could say things are getting pretty serious."

She laughed. "I'll join you two if there's room. I've got some dark chocolate in the kitchen. Do you want me to grab a bottle from the wine rack?"

He nodded. "I'll add an extra log to the fire." During other evenings, he and Mia had parted as soon as the kids were in bed. She had to get up early, and he enjoyed the quiet to check with his contacts and do some reading about parenting. So this was new.

A few minutes later, she carried in a tray of supplies. He opened the bottle and poured them each a glass. Without discussing it, they both sat on the floor in front of the hearth. It seemed a better choice than the couch for the evening.

"What should we talk about?" she asked after they'd clinked glasses and tasted the wine. It was a rich vintage, and he felt its warmth travel through his veins. That heat could be the company, too, he admitted. The flicker of firelight on Mia's skin was tantalizing. He needed to come up with a topic of conversation fast, or he'd start thinking about how her knit shirt showed off the swell of her breasts. Enough. He cut his thoughts off.

"How did you end up working at a bakery? Did you go to culinary school?" He had wondered about her history, and it seemed a safer topic than his contemplation of her figure.

"No." She shook her head. "I tried college, but I couldn't see spending the money when I didn't know what I wanted to do. So I left after a semester and began to wander. I took jobs that appealed to me and knocked around the country for several years."

"What was your favorite place?" Even though he'd never want a life like that, he was fascinated by it.

"Oh, I don't know." She broke off a couple of squares from the dark chocolate bar and handed one to him. "There have been a lot of interesting places. I think Savannah was my favorite city. It has a cool, laid-back vibe. And the tips were good." She raised her glass and took another sip of wine.

"Where did you work?" he asked to draw her out.

"Restaurants, mostly. I get the food business, and I love talking to people."

He could see that about her, even if he didn't have a similar ease around others. She had a way of making everyone feel comfortable.

"What about you?" She turned the question on him. "Did you plan to join the Navy after high school?"

"I made that decision when I was ten and set my sights on it. If I hadn't gotten into Annapolis, I'm not sure what I'd have done." That goal had controlled what he'd done throughout his youth, because he knew what it would take to be accepted: excellent grades, athletic skill, and self-discipline. He'd started talking to recruiters when he was fifteen.

"My guess is that there was no danger of you not getting in." She watched him over the rim of her wineglass.

"Probably not," he conceded. "I was focused."

"Was?" Her brows lifted. "I think you still are."

"Well, yeah. You've got to have a plan in life. That's how you get what you want." It was a lesson he'd learned early. His uncle Ned had a dream, but no plan to achieve it. When Kenton was nine, Uncle Ned had gone off to Nashville expecting to make it big in country music. He had talent, but no connections and no plan to make them. He just hoped to be "discovered." A year later, he'd come back, having gone through all his savings without ever achieving any success, and he had to live with Kenton's family until he could get back on his feet. It was partly Uncle Ned's example that had driven Kenton to be so regimented about his own future. That and the example set by his own parents.

"You mean like this house?" she asked.

"A solid home is important to me." He didn't add that the home was a foundational step in his life plan of home, wife, and kids.

"And you won't end up homeless like me," she quipped. He looked at her to assess her tone, but her poker face was in place.

"That apartment fire wasn't your fault," he said. Something like that could happen to anyone.

"No, but like other things, it set me in a different direction. I never know for sure what's coming next, and usually that's okay. I figure the universe gives me what I need when I need it. Losing my apartment meant I found my way here temporarily. Who knows where it will take me next?"

"What about the girls?" Having kids had to have changed her nomadic ways. Kids took planning.

"They're young enough to go with the flow. Once they get to be school age, I'll have to make decisions about where I want to be, but I have three or four years before I need to worry about that. Until then, I'm open to new experiences. Like meeting you," she added softly.

"Huh?" She was happy to have met him?

"I wouldn't have met you without the series of events that led me to your house."

Was it important to her that they'd met? He hadn't thought about the coincidence that had brought them together and given him a taste of raising kids. He couldn't have planned for that and wasn't sure how to respond, so he chose caution. "I hope it's been a good experience."

"It has. We're very different." She leaned back against a pillow. "But I like you."

"You sound surprised."

"I'm not," she said. "I've learned not to guess what people are like until I've met them. About you, based on your mother's words and what I saw in the house, I might have misjudged."

"How so?" He finished his wine and set it aside.

She smiled at him again. "I wouldn't have thought you were the type to sit on the floor and drink wine on a stormy evening."

He wouldn't have said that about himself, either, but there he was. The energy around them had changed, and it didn't have anything to do with the electric storm that had passed. "Am I the type who might kiss you?" The question was out before he could stop it.

"I don't have a type for that, but, as I said—" she twisted to place her wine glass on the hearth— "I welcome new experiences."

Kenton took that as invitation enough and reached for her. They'd shared two hugs, nice ones, but this moment was completely different. She wrapped her arms around his shoulders, and his went to her waist. They were still sitting on the floor but facing each other now. The fire crackled in the background, and the soft light picked up the colors in her hair. He coasted his hand through it, liking the way the shining waves filtered through his fingers.

"Do you have a kissing plan?" Her voice was light and teasing.

"Don't tempt me," he whispered as his mouth closed over hers. Some moments didn't require planning, and this was definitely one of those. He ran his tongue along her full bottom lip before delving into her mouth. She tasted of wine and chocolate and woman. Absolutely intoxicating.

Her fingers played against the skin of his neck and jaw as he deepened the kiss, their tongues tangling. When he broke away from her mouth, she lifted her chin, letting him know what she wanted. He wasted no time kissing down her neck until he nudged aside the top edge of her shirt to lick her collarbone. Her soft moan told him he'd found a spot she liked. Where else could he kiss her that would make her moan? He retraced his path back to her lips as his hands stroked the length of her back.

He was considering laying her down on his living room floor when a sharp crack of thunder made them break apart. Eliot jumped to his feet and began to bark, and the cry of a child from overhead reached them. Kissing was over for the night. Almost.

He cupped her cheek with his hand and placed one more soft kiss on her lips before rising and helping her to her feet.

10

M ia checked on the apple Danish baking in the oven. She'd had an unexpected day off, since the power remained out at the bakery. Fortunately, it was on at Kenton's home, so she and Kenton had cared for the girls, observing his time schedule during the morning and early afternoon. Then he'd retreated to his office and even missed dinner, and she had to wonder if he was avoiding her. She hoped the sugary scent of the Danish would draw him out, because they probably needed to have an adult conversation about the previous night's kissing.

Neither one of them had brought it up, even when they'd had a minute or two during the day when the girls were occupied. Did his silence mean he was regretting it? She hoped not, because she sure wasn't. Those kisses had been among the best she'd experienced, and she couldn't quite say why. Was it because Kenton kissed like he did everything else, with serious intention, even if there hadn't been a plan? Or was he just a great kisser?

She wasn't sure, but she hoped to get the opportunity to find out.

"Eat?" Emma danced around Mia's feet as she removed the pastries from the oven.

"They'll be too hot, but you can have one in the morning for breakfast. I promise." She'd leave a note for Kenton. He'd probably object to the sweet at the morning meal due to the lack of nutritional value, but Mia kept her promises to the girls. "Bedtime for you two. Up we go."

Mia let the twins play in the bathtub to wear them out before tucking them into their cribs. She knew they'd talk with each other before going to sleep, but that was good for them. Twins usually had a language of their own, and these two were no different. Their speech patterns were just developing, but she'd noticed both verbal and nonverbal communication between them.

Before leaving their room, she adjusted the nanny cam in the corner and checked to make sure it was connected to her phone.

"Night night," she said, giving them each a kiss before closing their door and going downstairs.

She entered the empty living room that was remarkably clutter-free, since they'd followed Kenton's rules about cleaning up after play. It was all in the schedule, but it meant that Mia had nothing she had to do. She could bake more or start laundry, but neither of those options sounded as good as rousting Kenton from his lair. She turned her head to look toward his office door.

But she needed to set the stage. The storms the day before had ushered in fall-like temperatures, so a fire might be nice and romantic. She piled wood and kindling in the fireplace and had a fire going in no time. With that done, she headed for the kitchen.

Wine or something else? The colder air had her thinking about a warm beverage. Irish coffee seemed perfect. In the kitchen, she started a fresh pot of coffee brewing while she got out the whiskey and brown sugar and whipped up some heavy cream. She assembled the drinks in glass mugs, dusted a dash of cocoa powder on top, and carried them to Kenton's office.

"Knock, knock," she said and nudged open the door. "I brought you something, but I'd like to entice you to come out of here."

He glanced up from where he sat in front of his computer screen with a pen in one hand and a notepad nearby.

"Please," she added, hoping to recall him from the thoughts that appeared to take him miles away.

"You're right." With a sigh, he put the pen down and closed the lid of his laptop. "I've been in here too long. The girls?"

"Already in bed. Irish coffee?" She handed him a mug.

He grinned at her suddenly. "What makes you think I'm Irish?"

"It might be the Fitzpatrick part of your name. Not that it matters when it comes to liking this drink. I'm not Irish, and it's one of my favorite treats." She waited for him to take a sip before continuing. "I started a fire. Will you join me?"

She didn't wait for him to respond but walked toward the living room. The office door closed, and she heard his footsteps following her. When she sat on the couch, she patted the seat next to her. He was still tense, probably from what he had or hadn't discovered while in his office. Maybe if she got him to talk about it, he could move past it so they could enjoy the evening. And kiss some more, which she admitted was her main motivation.

"Learn anything new?" She didn't know exactly what he was doing in there, but she guessed it had to do with the assailant who had come after them.

He shook his head as he sat next to her on the couch. "Analyzing my last mission again. I'm still trying to figure out where it went wrong."

"And you think the threat against us is connected to it?" He'd told her about the mission and conveyed his concerns about how it might be the source of the threat, but she hadn't asked too many questions.

"I'm convinced of it, but my CO thinks differently." His fist was balled up on his thigh. "I need something to present to him that will make him re-evaluate the situation. It might be the only way to eliminate the threat."

"You have access to the mission records even off base?" Mia didn't know much about the military or what he did, but that struck her as odd.

"Intelligence sent me a secure link to the database where the records are stored. They thought it might help me figure out the current threat. I just keep going over that mission, and I can't pinpoint where it went sideways." His face was intense, and she could imagine how he might look in the field. "Everything was planned down to the minute, and I can't find fault with the execution, but still the leader slipped past us."

"What if your CO is right, and the threat has nothing to do with that mission?" she suggested.

"I still want to know what happened." He unfisted his hand and rubbed it over his leg. "Another SEAL team has been deployed on a cleanup mission. I might be able to help them."

They sat in silence for a few minutes as they both sipped their drinks. The coffee had cooled to the perfect temperature, and she was searching for just the right words to say to him. Nothing came to her, so she went with honesty. "Have you ever thought that you carry too many burdens?"

"What?" He seemed shocked by her question. "No. It's my job. It's what I do. My team depends on me to do my part, and somehow I failed at that despite the best-laid plans."

"We all fail sometimes." She kept her voice gentle.

"Failures like that cost lives," he argued.

"Were any of your guys harmed?" she asked. She hadn't gotten the impression that had been the case.

"No," he admitted, "but I've left someone free in the world who has a history of harming others, particularly children. I can't live with that." He was a serious man, and she admired him for that, but he had to realize that he couldn't carry the weight of the world around with him.

"But there's another team out looking for him," Mia said, hoping to remove some of his guilt, "so it's not your problem anymore."

"That's not how it works with the SEALs." He leaned back and rested his head against the cushion.

"That would be too much responsibility for me." With her nieces to raise, she had to look at the world differently, but what he took on was too much. "I think I'll stick to baking, where a failure means the dough didn't rise or the cake icing was too thick."

"Can you fix those problems?" He turned his head and looked at her.

"The icing, yes, but not the dough. It gets tossed in the trash can. Ultimately, no harm is done," she said. "I'm willing to bet you've done more good than harm on your missions. I would even guess that all the others have been successes. Am I right?"

He didn't answer for a minute. "Some have gone better than others, but, yeah, it's fair to say I have a record of success."

"Focusing on that might make *these* better." She touched the wrinkles that cut across his forehead and smoothed them out with her fingertips. "And a little whiskey helps most situations. Drink up."

"Yes, ma'am." He raised his mug to his lips and drained it. She took it from him and placed it with hers on the coffee table. When she turned back, his hand found hers, and he laced their fingers together. "I didn't ask how the rest of your day was."

"No problems to report." As a matter of fact, when he touched her, she could hardly remember anything about her day. She wanted to scoot into his lap and kiss the daylights out of him, but his emotions still seemed a little raw, so she let him set the pace. He raised their joined hands to his mouth and brushed his lips across the back of her hand, sending shivers of desire up her arm. Maybe slow was a good thing.

"I've been thinking about our kiss last night," he surprised her by saying.

"Oh?" She contained her response, though she really wanted to ask if it had meant something to him?

"You haven't?" Hurt flickered through his eyes.

"Only all day," she said with a smile. "It was good."

His return smile was slow and sexy. "I think we can do better."

Better? That seemed difficult to believe, but she was willing to try if he was. And all signs suggested he was.

"Wait." She pressed her free hand against his chest. His very muscular chest. "Have you been planning another kiss?"

He cocked his head. "I'd be lying if I said no, but in my head it wasn't just a kiss. Come closer."

She scooted toward him with no hesitation until she was straddling his lap and they were lip to lip. "Good?"

"Perfect." His hands were already slipping under the edge of her shirt. "You're beautiful. That was my first thought about you."

"When I was jabbing you in the gut with your own baseball bat?" She didn't mention how hot she'd thought him during that same encounter.

"Even then." He leaned closer and let his lips wander up her neck. He'd done that the night before, and it felt just as good now. "No moan tonight?"

She laughed against his temple. "I'm trying to seem sophisticated."

"I'd rather you be you. Full of life, spontaneous, sexy."

She took his face in her hands and looked into his eyes, and she saw what she needed to. His words were a compliment, and he wanted her as much as she wanted him. "Okay. My spontaneous side says we should take this upstairs to a bed."

"My bed. It's bigger," he said, standing up and taking her with him. She wrapped her legs around his waist and hung on, liking the feel of his hands on her butt to keep her balanced as he went up the steps.

He turned into the master bedroom and lowered her feet to the floor, letting her slide down him. Through his jeans, she could feel his erection against her. She had just time to process that when he began a kiss that left her breathless. He broke the kiss to pull her shirt over her head before going back to it. She tugged at his clothing, wanting to feel his skin on hers.

She pulled back from the kiss long enough to say, "Clothes off." He unfastened her bra, and she shimmied out of it. His hands cupped her breasts, lifting them together, as he lowered his head to kiss the top curve of each one almost reverently. She wanted to crawl out of her skin and into his. But his was still covered. "I meant you, too."

"Happy to." He took a step back and stripped off his shirt, which was quickly followed by his jeans and boxers. He was beautiful, male perfection with ripples of muscle covering his large frame. A few scars marred his skin but enhanced his masculinity. And he was hard. Just for her. "Now you."

"Huh?" She'd been so busy gawking at him that she didn't understand his words.

"Take the rest of your clothes off, sweetheart. I want to see all of you." He put his hands on his hips and waited.

She pushed her yoga pants down, catching her panties with her thumbs as she went, and stepped out of both. The air was cool around her, but his gaze was hot, warming her.

"Get in bed." His voice had dropped to a commanding growl. She considered disobeying to see what would happen, but she decided she could comply just this once.

So she flipped back the covers and climbed in while he killed the bright overhead light and turned on a small lamp on the dresser. Mood lighting. He was setting the stage. And the stage was his very large bed. He came toward her, and she liked everything she saw. Before joining her, he set a condom on the bedside table.

"I have more if we need them," he said.

She wanted to tease him about always being prepared, but it wasn't the time. "Good. Come here."

He covered her body with his, balancing on his forearms to keep his weight off her but letting their bodies touch, which was glorious. His erection pressed into her stomach as he started another kiss. God, he was good at that. Soon their bodies were moving together. Even before he entered her, they found a rhythm to please them both.

She almost objected when he broke the kiss, but he put his lips to good use, catching the nipple of one breast in his mouth. His fingers played with the other, and renewed heat shot through her. He knew how to touch her, and then his lips were moving again, tracing a path over her stomach.

"Do you like to be licked here?" He didn't wait for an answer before dipping his tongue between her thighs.

"God, yes," she whispered, her hands going into his hair and smoothing out the dark waves. His day-old beard scraped against her tender skin, but it only added to the sensations he was creating with his mouth. She couldn't stop herself from arching up and spreading her legs wider. She felt herself begin to unravel but didn't want to come without him. "Inside me."

"With pleasure," he murmured against her cunt, his hot breath a caress. He came back over her and reached for the condom, efficiently tearing it open and rolling it on himself. She wanted to offer to help, but she liked watching his confident movements.

"You made quick work of that," she said as he settled back over her.

"I'm motivated. Wrap your legs around me." He kissed her then, his tongue delving deeply into her mouth as he entered her.

She felt almost overwhelmed by the size of him, but he pushed in slowly, giving her body time to adjust to him, until he was fully inside her and she clenched her muscles around him.

"Jesus. Mia, that's…" He didn't finish his sentence. He didn't need to. He was showing her with his body how he felt. The tension built between them as he thrust in, deep then shallow, deep then shallow. It was driving her wild as she hovered on the edge of an orgasm.

"Now, Kenton. Please." Her voice was a throaty whisper, but he heard her and pushed in deeper and faster. Seconds later, she came, her entire body shivering with her release. He thrust once more, his head buried against her shoulder.

"So damn good," he said as he stilled. His lips moved against her throat before finding their way upward to her mouth. His kiss was gentle now, soothing, not arousing. He kissed her cheeks, her temples, and smoothed her hair back from her face.

She'd never felt so... what was the word? Loved? No, not that. Couldn't be that. Cherished. There, that was better. The feeling remained while he slept next to her, their bodies still touching.

11

Mia rolled over in bed and encountered a large, sprawled-out body. She blinked and woke up fully. Her nose was inches from Kenton's shoulder. In the dim light, she could make out his profile and see the steady rise and fall of his chest. Memories of the previous evening flooded back.

He'd been upset about his perceived failure, but the sex hadn't been about cheering him up. It had been something they both wanted. And it had been amazing. Probably the best of her life.

"Ever woken up with a man before?" His voice was gravelly with sleep.

"Not very often." Hardly ever. She'd had casual relationships, but those didn't include staying the night with a guy. With Kenton, she'd felt no need to return to her room down the hall. She'd have been unhappy if he'd asked her to.

His arm slid under her, lifting her so that she lay on top of him. "Then you probably don't know that men wake up hard a lot of mornings."

She squirmed against him, feeling his arousal. "I thought that was for me."

"Trust me, it is, sweetheart." His hands stroked down her back to cup her butt.

She laughed and dropped a kiss on his chest, liking where this seemed to be going, but… "The girls will be awake soon."

"Then we'd better be quick," he said. His eyes were as intense as when they first met, but the promise in them now wasn't danger. It was something much more stimulating.

"Not too quick," she cautioned as she took him inside her.

Ten minutes later, she was collapsed on top of him. She decided that quick with him was better than slow with anyone else. His fingers were lazily trailing down her back while they caught their breath. She propped her chin on his chest and studied his face. He seemed deep in thought about something.

"What are you thinking?" she asked.

"That it's a good day to start potty training the girls," he said.

"What?" Her brain was still foggy with sex and sleep. She couldn't have heard him right.

"The girls are ready." He sounded so sure that she lifted herself over him and looked down into his face.

"And how would you know that?" She hadn't even considered the concept yet. She figured the girls would let her know when they wanted to use the potty.

"I read what the signs are." His voice was confident.

Of course he had. "In your book?"

"That's right." He grinned at her. "And I hate changing diapers."

"Ah, the truth comes out." She chuckled.

He quirked up an eyebrow. "Do you enjoy it?"

"Nope," she admitted. "I suppose it won't hurt to try, and since we're both home today, we can keep an eye on them." She pushed herself up all the way. "I'm game, I guess, but I need a shower and coffee before I can think about it too much."

His hands stayed on her hips. "The shower in the master bathroom is big," he suggested. "Really big."

That was an invitation her spontaneous side would love to accept, but she couldn't, at least not at that moment. "If we get in there together, we'll never hear the girls when they wake." Her imagination was already taking off in directions it shouldn't, involving him and the large shower.

He groaned, his fingers idly playing with her nipples. "This parenting thing has limitations."

"Sometimes, but they're sweethearts. You've got to admit that. We'll save shower sex for another time." She kissed him hard on the lips before rolling off him and out of bed, where she felt suddenly self-conscious. That wasn't like her, but, she admitted, she wasn't used to waking up with a guy and she didn't have a robe to cover herself. He was propped on his elbows, watching her as she stood naked and indecisive in his room.

"Wear my shirt," he suggested, coming to her rescue. "It'll be plenty big."

She snatched the shirt from the floor where it had landed the night before and tugged it over her head. It was huge, covering her to mid-thigh, but best of all it carried his scent.

"Looks good on you." His eyes skimmed over her, and she felt a rush of heat. "Come give me another kiss."

She laughed. "We'll never get this day started if I do that. See you at breakfast," she said and scooted from the room. The girls were chatting in their bed, but they seemed content enough, so she went past their room and got a quick shower.

Even so, Kenton beat her downstairs and had the twins in the kitchen by the time she was ready. They were sitting in their high chairs eating apple Danish while he explained about potty training.

She nodded in support of what he said when they looked to her, but inside she was laughing. It was funny to watch the big, sexy SEAL explain about using the potty. He laid out the advantages to them, selling them on the point of getting pretty underpants. He must have read that in his book, but it made her think about her own lingerie. The apartment fire had wiped out anything she had that was nice, and she hadn't restocked, since she'd deemed it unlikely that there would be a man in her life anytime soon.

Was he in her life?

Mia poured a cup of coffee and considered it. He seemed to be, but she had no reason to believe that it was anything but the kind of affair that happened because of proximity and attraction. She could be okay with that, she guessed, since she doubted she fit into the plans Kenton no doubt had for himself.

Enjoy the moment, the voice in her head told her. She'd always been good at that and didn't see why it should change.

After breakfast, they gave each girl a turn on the potty and practiced flushing it, even tossing in Cheerios so they could watch them swirl around and go down. Throughout the day, they took the girls to the bathroom and encouraged them.

If Kenton felt ridiculous cheering for a little girl to go pee in the potty, it didn't show. He took this as seriously as he did everything else. He went by the book and kept it structured, but success or failure also depended on the girls dictating what they needed, which suited Mia's philosophy of parenting. It was a good compromise, and if it meant not changing diapers, she was all in.

At bedtime and after just one accident during the day, Mia declared the experiment a success. She had no doubt that there would be setbacks and more accidents, but the girls had taken an important step forward. When she came downstairs after making sure they were settled for the night, Kenton was waiting for her. He didn't speak but wrapped her in his arms and held her against him. She breathed in the scent of his skin. They hadn't touched throughout the day, not wanting the girls to ask questions, and she'd missed him even if they had been in the same house.

"What should we do to celebrate a successful day?" he said against her hair a few minutes later.

She tilted her head up to see his face. "You don't have a plan?"

He kissed her lips before responding. "Well, I do, but…"

"Tell me," she said.

He leaned closer and whispered in her ear. His description of exactly what he wanted to do with her in the shower was intimate and detailed enough to make her blush. And about the most delightful way she could think of to spend her evening. She broke away from him, took his hand, and led him up the stairs.

12

Kenton paced through the house, cleaning even where there wasn't dirt. He was tired of being stuck in the house, even a bit jealous that Mia was still going out to work. She'd gone in early that day, whispering when she slipped out of his arms at three in the morning that she'd be home by noon. He'd missed her warmth and her curvy body next to his.

The nights had been the best part of the past five days. Nights they spent in his bed. They'd gotten in the habit of turning in early to make love and talk until falling asleep. He had no complaints about any of that. But this waiting around for the other shoe to drop needed to end. He was feeling cooped up, and he thought the girls were, too. He'd allowed them into the backyard, but not beyond, fearing that something might happen to them.

"I'm home," Mia called from the front door.

Thank god was Kenton's immediate reaction as the girls rushed to greet their aunt. She swung each of them up and kissed their cheeks. He'd like to kiss her, but they were still being careful to keep their displays of affection to a minimum in front of the kids.

"How's the day been?" she asked him with a smile.

"Nothing to complain about," he responded, but her eyes were on him. She wasn't quite sold. "I need to work in my office for a bit. Can you…"

"Sure. Come on, girls. I want to tell you about the most beautiful dog I saw today." She took them into the living room, leaving him standing by the front door, dissatisfied.

He shook it off and headed for his office. His CO had promised an update, even though it was Saturday. Kenton had just enough time to connect to the video chat before it started. Giving Patrick and Anderson a quick nod, he turned his attention to Colonel Schaffer, who got down to business immediately.

"We've confirmed the attack on you was posted on a kind of mercenary job board. Unfortunately, we haven't yet pinpointed who placed it. Either way, the job, if you will, is listed again, so we're assuming the original group failed and it's open to other mercenary groups. Whoever is after you has increased the price they're willing to pay and the seriousness of the job. It's being listed as an actual contract now."

Kenton sucked in a breath and tried not to look rattled. Putting a contract on someone usually meant these groups were looking to kill or capture. Did they want just him? Or were Mia and the girls equally at risk?

"Do you have any details, colonel?" he recovered enough to ask.

"No, captain, and I know what you're thinking. It's still safest to keep the woman and kids with you for the moment. The good news is that the latest intelligence says the contract is untaken. You've got some breathing space, but don't let your guard down." The colonel turned his attention to Anderson and Patrick. "Gentleman, I'll need you to begin pulling guard duty as well. You can hold off until we have confirmation that someone has taken the contract. It probably won't be long. You doing all right, Fitzpatrick?"

"Yes, sir." Kenton kept his composure. "I appreciate the information."

"Keep in touch," the colonel said, ending the call for everyone.

"Shit," Kenton muttered. "Shit, shit, shit." That was about the worst news he could have gotten. The only glimmer of positivity was that no one was trying to get to them that day… probably. It was small consolation. Should he tell Mia how serious their situation was? He'd likely have to, because some things were going to need to change.

The shriek of little girls sounded from outside his office. Even the heavy oak door couldn't keep it out entirely. The doorknob turned, and he heard Mia's voice.

"No, Emma, don't bother him."

"I want Kenton." Despite his ill humor, he almost smiled. Emma could be counted on to be persistent. He had to admit to a fondness for her attitude, and Ava was warm and loving. Both the girls were appealing in their individual ways. And their aunt held all sorts of appeal.

"It's okay. You can come in," he called through the door.

"Sorry," Mia said, coming in with both girls. "They're restless today."

"Been that way since they got up," he said.

"Maybe a walk to the park," Mia suggested. "It's beautiful outside, and they've hardly…" She trailed off, watching him closely. Emma held her arms up to him. He lifted her onto his knee while he stroked Ava's hair, but Mia must have seen something in his expression. "What's the matter, Kenton?"

"Nothing new," he said. He'd known in his gut that someone was out to harm them since the initial attack, and whoever it was wouldn't be satisfied with a scare or threat.

"Okay, but you look—"

"Outside," Emma yanked on his arm. "We want outside." Ava took hold of his other hand and tugged.

Kenton should say no, but he got where they were coming from. He was tired of being cooped up as well. And, he reasoned, an attack wasn't imminent. After today he wouldn't be sure of that, and he'd have to keep them on lockdown.

"How about a drive?" he suggested. They could stay in his truck, which gave him the capacity to get away quickly if he needed to elude an attacker.

More little-girl shrieks sounded while Emma and Ava danced around him in their excitement.

"I'll pack a bag," Mia said, looking pleased.

"We won't be gone long," he warned. An hour tops. He would pick a country road, maybe see some fall colors, and be home in no time.

"It's good to be prepared." She flashed him a grin, probably enjoying tossing his number one personality trait back at him.

"Meet at the door in twenty minutes," he said, standing up and putting Emma on her feet. The girls dashed off, chattering with each other.

"Thanks." Mia lingered. "Are you sure nothing's wrong?"

He shook his head but couldn't resist opening his arms to her. She came to him, putting her arms around his waist and resting her head against him. He didn't know if she was seeking comfort or giving it. Either way, he was glad to hold her. After a minute, he dropped a kiss on her hair and pulled back.

"We better find them," he quipped, "or they'll be out the door without us."

Twenty minutes later they were in his truck making their way out of town. He'd picked a route that would take them through scenic, hilly country and a couple of quaint small towns. In his head, he mapped out a circuit that would take about an hour. When they returned, he'd call Patrick and Anderson and plan a schedule of protection for his household. He hated doing that to his buddies when they wanted to spend time with their families, but he knew they'd do anything to help him keep Mia and the girls safe.

"Look, girls, cows." Mia pointed out the window at a field. "What do cows say?"

"Moo," Ava answered, making the sound stretch out.

"That's right. Oh, and there are horses. See how pretty they are when they run."

They were passing a fenced area where a half dozen horses raced across a pasture. Kenton slowed the truck so the girls could get a better view.

"Horsey," the girls cried in unison, excited about seeing the animals.

Mia's hand crept across the seat to touch his leg. He reached down to clasp her fingers between his. This short drive was making the girls so happy, and he felt almost comfortable. He'd kept his eyes on the rearview mirror. No vehicles appeared to be following them.

"What's this?" Mia exclaimed as they crested a rise and entered the outskirts of a small town. People were parked along the streets, and families headed in the direction of a park. A banner stretched across the road announced, The Country Pumpkin Patch. "It's a festival. Can we stop? Just for a few minutes. It would be so much fun for the girls."

He hesitated, not wanting to disappoint her or the twins but reluctant to put them at risk.

"Stop, stop," the twins chanted from the back seat.

When a car pulled out of a space just ahead, he took it as a sign from the universe and parked his truck, deciding that they could take the afternoon to enjoy themselves. He helped Mia get the girls out of their car seats, and they joined hands to cross the street. As they headed into the festival grounds, they blended in with other families, not that it took Kenton's mind off his need to protect them.

"Pumpkin painting over there," Mia said, scanning the area, "and games, food, crafts. There's something for everyone. Where should we start?"

Emma and Ava were wide eyed, taking it all in and ready to run in every direction. Kenton tightened his grip on Emma's hand when she started to pull away.

"One thing at a time, kiddo," he said to her.

Mia chose the games area first, where the girls tried to toss a ring around the stem of a pumpkin, used a net to fish for apples in a big tub, and ran through a maze made from hay bales stacked two high. It was easy for Kenton to keep track of their movements from the outside, but they couldn't see over the bales, making the maze fun for them. When their cheeks were pink with exertion, Mia suggested food and drinks. They purchased delicious apple fritters and washed them down with cold cider.

The only potential danger Kenton could see came from the honeybees that were also drawn to the sweets. He kept his eye on the crowd, but no one stood out. Everyone looked like what they were: parents and grandparents with glee-filled little kids.

Mia popped the last of her fritter in her mouth and bent to wipe sugar from the girls' hands, giving Kenton a view he appreciated down her blouse. Her body was curvy and beautiful, and she neither flaunted it nor tried to hide it, which he liked.

"Hey," she said, taking a swipe at him with the napkin when she realized where his gaze had gone. "This is a PG event."

"Sorry, but I can't resist beauty like that." He kept his voice low enough not to be heard by the exuberant crowd around them.

"Later, you won't have to," she said with a flirtatious smile.

It struck him how easy it was to imagine that this was all real, that they were a family like the ones around them. The way they had come together didn't fit in with his plan for himself, but he was starting to wonder how much his plan mattered.

"Pretty." Ava pointed to floral wreaths for sale in a nearby booth.

"Those are very pretty," Mia agreed. "We should look at the crafts. Okay with you?" Mia's question pulled his thoughts back to the moment.

"We can stay a little longer." He realized in that moment it would be tough to deny them anything.

A half hour later, that theory was tested when Mia wanted to stay to watch a folk music group perform. He'd noticed that the festival grounds had gotten more crowded, with everyone making their way toward a stage at one end. The singing group must have been popular, judging by the number of people.

Mia lightly touched his arm and leaned closer into him. The girls were at their feet, tucked between them.

"I know you didn't want to stay this long, but can we listen to part of

the concert?" she asked. "Please. It's been such a good day. I don't
want to go home yet."

He hesitated. They'd already spent almost two hours there, but then
he looked down at Emma's and Ava's sweet faces, and couldn't say
no. "We'll stay a little longer."

They moved closer to the stage area and found a spot on the grass to
sit. During the first two songs, the girls danced and twirled around
them, clearly enjoying the music.

"Okay, all you kiddies out there," the lead singer called as the next
song started, "the band needs some help with this one. Who wants to
come up and play an instrument with us?" Stage assistants brought
out baskets filled with little drums, triangles, and maracas. Perfect for
small hands.

"Can we?" Emma spoke first.

"I don't see why not," Mia answered before Kenton could, but she
glanced at him. He gave her a nod of confirmation, since the girls
wouldn't be out of their sight.

The girls held hands and went up the steps to the stage. Emma boldly
headed to the center and grabbed instruments for each of them, then
took a spot near Ava at the stage's edge.

"Oh, they're so cute," Mia exclaimed, digging through her shoulder
bag. "Where's my phone? I want a picture. Would you check in the
diaper bag for it?"

The diaper bag was a backpack that Kenton had carried. He opened
the largest compartment and peered inside, moving items around to
see under them.

"Here it is," she said excitedly. "I must have missed it."

Kenton saw Mia's profile when she focused back in on the stage. Her jaw dropped, and she leaped to her feet a second later. He turned his attention to where the twins should be, and a sick feeling hit his stomach. Ava wasn't there.

"Ava's gone!" Mia leaped to her feet and ran for the stage, but he stayed where he was, studying the crowd. If someone had snatched the girl, they couldn't have gone far. His eyes narrowed, looking for Ava's blonde curls and pink jacket. He caught a glimpse of Mia reaching a now-crying Emma and scooping her up.

One twin safe. He started moving toward the only entrance to the stage area. The sides were fenced off with hay bales. An adult could easily go over them, but that might attract attention. Kenton's money was on someone trying to look like a parent working his way toward the exit. That's how he'd play it if he were trying to kidnap a child at a festival.

Kenton moved out onto the festival grounds, his head snapping from side to side as he continued to search. The thought that Ocampa must be behind this hovered at the fringes of his thoughts, raising his pulse rate. Kidnapping a child was right up his alley. Kenton couldn't think about that yet. He had a mission to perform.

"Too damn many kids," he muttered but kept his focus sharp. His concentration paid off when he caught a flash of pink twenty yards ahead. A man, dressed to blend in in jeans and a hoodie, was carrying a crying child toward the parking lot. "Shit, no." If they reached a vehicle, Kenton would have a hell of a time catching them.

Kenton charged ahead, vaguely aware of people scattering in front of him until he was only a few yards from the man.

"Stop! Put her down!" Kenton yelled in a booming voice. The crowd around him paused as he knew they would, the volume of voices dropping. "Kidnapper!"

The man turned his attention on Kenton, who was barreling closer. Kenton saw the man evaluate his choices. He could drop the kid and possibly get away or stay and end up fighting Kenton. The man opened his arms and let Ava slump to the ground before running toward a white van.

Kenton wanted in the worst way to chase the guy down and pound him into the ground, but Ava was sobbing where she'd fallen. Was she hurt? Only scared? Kenton picked her up and held her close to him, rubbing her back and murmuring soothing words. He looked up in time to get the van's license plate before it pulled out onto the road and was gone.

"It's okay, little one," he said. "I've got you." Ava's short arms went around his neck as she sobbed into his shoulder.

A hand touched his arm. "Everything okay, mister? Was that guy trying to take your kid?"

"Yeah, we're all right now. Thanks," Kenton said to the man who had approached him.

"I wouldn't have expected that kind of thing to happen here." The guy seemed stunned.

"Custody issue," Kenton said to defuse the situation. Such battles could get ugly and lead to kidnappings by one or the other parent. He didn't want the festival to erupt in panic due to what appeared to be a random kidnapping attempt. Nothing about it had been random, and the other festivalgoers had nothing to fear.

"Do you have her?" Mia rushed up, carrying Emma. "Oh, thank god. Is she all right?"

"Just scared, I think," Kenton said, trading twins with Mia. Emma was crying, too, but Ava needed the reassurances that only her aunt could give her. "We need to get out of here."

"Yes, right away," Mia agreed.

They made their way to his truck. Once he got them in and situated, he took a minute to check the most likely places on the undercarriage for a tracking device. No one had followed them, of that he was sure, but someone knew where they were. It didn't take him long to find the small tracker on the inside of a fender well.

"Son of a bitch." Kenton could have kicked himself. The device hadn't even been well hidden, but he hadn't thought to check for it. He ripped it off and popped out the tiny battery that powered it. Everything in him wanted to crush the device to smithereens beneath his heel, but he didn't. Identifying the manufacturer might help point them to who placed it, so he shoved it in his pocket.

When he got in the truck, Mia was sitting in the back seat between the girls. No one was crying anymore, but the atmosphere was heavy with fear.

"I'm sorry, Mia," he said, starting the vehicle.

"It's not your fault." Her fingers touched his shoulder, but he shrugged her off.

"Like hell it isn't," he muttered in a low voice as he pulled out on the road and headed for home.

13

When they reached home, Kenton was torn between hustling Mia and the girls into the house and taking the time to make sure it was safe. Recognizing that he couldn't leave them sitting ducks in the driveway, he took them up to the master bedroom and told them to stay put.

A search of the house and a check of the security system revealed nothing, so he returned to the bedroom. Mia put her finger over her lips when he opened the door. Both girls were asleep on the bed, curled into each other. They looked sweet and fragile, reminding him again of the weight of his responsibilities.

"I need to check in with my team," Kenton said in a low voice when Mia rested her head against his chest. He held her for a minute before breaking away. Before leaving the room, he opened his top dresser drawer and pulled out a whistle. "If you need me, blow this."

"I'm sure that's not necessary," she said, lifting her face to his and letting him see how troubled her eyes were. Later, he'd comfort her the best he could, but he had duties first.

"Just keep it with you." He pushed it into her hand and made his way to his office to boot up his computer. His plan was to contact his CO first, but an email from an unknown sender caught his eye. The subject line read *Next Time*. With a sinking feeling, he opened the email. It contained one sentence.

We will succeed in taking everyone you hold dear.

The message, time-stamped twenty minutes earlier, needed no interpretation, but it sent a jolt to Kenton's heart. When Mia and the girls had first been threatened, he'd had some distance and perspective. They were little more than strangers to him. After living with them and growing emotionally closer, he recognized that he did hold them dear. They were in his life temporarily, and neither he nor Mia expected more, but he'd be damned if they'd be harmed while he was protecting them.

Controlling his anger, he logged into the secure system that allowed him to speak with his CO so he could explain what had happened that afternoon. Next, he forwarded the email to the Navy techs so they could attempt to trace it. He figured that was futile, but you never knew.

Finally, he took another good, hard look at his home's security system, assessing it for ways to beef it up. He adjusted camera angles and changed access codes. When he'd done everything he could think to do, he went in search of Mia and found her in the laundry room off the kitchen. The girls were in their high chairs a few feet away, eating dinner.

"More laundry?" It seemed endless.

"Accident," she said, as she added fabric softener to the washer. "Both of them."

"What? No way." He kept his tone low. "They were doing so well." Could nothing go right today?

"Today was traumatic." Ava turned on the machine. "And I told you there were going to be accidents, and we have to be okay with that."

"No reason for it," he insisted.

Mia sighed. "Kenton, you can't take such a hard line on potty training. It'll happen when it happens."

That was her theory, but he'd proven pretty effectively that he'd been right about the timing. The girls had been ready, and they'd been great until today.

He ran a hand through his hair. Maybe he shouldn't be worrying about this now, when they had bigger problems. Mia was leaning against the dryer with her arms crossed, and he guessed she was thinking the same thing.

"Did you learn anything new?" She looked tired and worried.

"Not much new," he said, opting to keep the email to himself. "It's safe to assume that we're being watched at all times."

"More than a tracker on your truck?" She had to know the answer to her own question.

"Much more, I suspect," he said. "We have to be careful, Mia. Very careful."

"Aunt Mia," one of the girls called. "I want you in here."

"Be right there, sweetie," Mia called as she pushed off the dryer.

He caught her arm when she passed by him. "We'll talk later."

"Sure," she said, giving him a half-hearted smile.

As soon as she walked away, his phone rang, and he checked the screen. His mother. He wasn't in the mood, but she would just keep calling if he ignored her.

"Hi, Mom," he said.

"Kenton. I'm glad I caught you," she said. "Your father and I were thinking of stopping over to see you."

"It's not a good time," he responded. The last thing he wanted was to drag his parents into this mess. They had a good security system on their home, but he'd check with his CO about getting some protection assigned to them. If nothing else, the local PD might be willing to increase their patrols in his parents' neighborhood. "I'm sorry, but things are complicated."

"How so?" Instant concern showed in her voice.

"I'd prefer not to get into it." He hoped that would be enough to put his mom off.

"Are Mia and the girls still with you?"

"Yes, they're here, and they're fine," he said, anticipating her next question. "We're just really busy at the moment trying to potty train the girls." It was a half-truth, which was good enough in the current situation, he decided.

"That can be a challenge," his mother said sympathetically. "But I don't see why—"

"From what I've read, it's best not to disrupt their schedules during the early phases." He wasn't lying; he had read that.

"Sure, I can see that," she agreed, "but we'd like to have you all over for dinner soon."

He wanted to say that he, Mia, and the girls were not a family unit, and he hoped his mother wasn't thinking in that direction.

"That sounds nice, Mom. I've got to go. Love to Dad," he said and hung up. His mother was going to think he was acting abnormally, and she'd be right. But it was her doing that Mia and the kids were living in his house, after all. What his mother and her damned hospitality couldn't have foreseen was the danger she had inadvertently put his guests in.

～

"Victory!" Kenton declared when he came down the steps after putting the twins to bed.

"How so? Are they already asleep?" Mia struggled up from the couch where she'd dropped in exhaustion after finishing the laundry and cleaning up from dinner. The day had been emotionally draining, and she could barely keep her eyes open.

"Not quite, but Emma pooped in the potty." He sounded very pleased with himself.

"That's good," she said, pretending enthusiasm. It was impossible to be excited about anything when she thought back over the day. She had almost lost Ava. What if she never saw her shy, sweet niece again? Mia shuddered. She'd lost so many family members. Her parents, her sister, and her brother-in-law. The thought of something happening to one of the twins made her insides quake.

"It's fantastic," he said, apparently not picking up on her mood. "We're almost there."

"Kenton," she said, bringing him back down. "I'm happy about it, too, but... today." She squeezed her eyes shut, trying to negate the sick fear that swamped her.

"I know, sweetheart, but Ava's okay."

"For today." She opened her eyes and focused on him. "For tonight, maybe. But what about tomorrow? Do you know who is after us, and why? Where is this going to end?"

He sat down next to her, his greater weight making her lean toward him on the couch, but she pulled back when he tried to put his arm around her shoulders. Several beats of silence passed before he spoke. "Mercenaries have been hired to come after us."

Mercenaries? Didn't that sort of thing only happen in movies? "Us? The girls and I have nothing to do with—"

"I know, but you live in my house, and we've been watched," he said. She could see by the way his jaw tightened that he hated to admit that. "They've seen the two of us together and me with the girls and have drawn conclusions. I had a threat via email today when we got home."

"Oh, god," she whispered, putting her hands over her face. "I thought it was bad, but…" She knew her words were muffled, but she didn't want him to see the tears in her eyes.

"Hey, I'm as worried as you are," he said softly, pulling her hands from her face, "but we'll get through this together."

She blinked back the tears. "You think so?"

"I do. Patrick and Anderson are going to be guarding the exterior in shifts. That gives us another layer of protection. I know it feels awful to be just sitting around, but trust me, we'll be okay."

Mia gulped in air, trying to calm her nerves. She knew she had to trust him to be right in this situation, since she was way out of her league, but it was tough to depend on him. That wasn't who she was. She figured things out as she went—and on her own, generally. But she had him now, even if it was temporary.

Kenton was watching her closely. When she met his eyes, he lifted her hands to his lips and kissed her palms. His small action sent a wave of desire through her.

"Come to bed with me," he said. "We'll do things that will take your worries away."

Despite her fears, she laughed. They had that between them. The physical side of things was good. Maybe she could forget about the day, just for a little while, if they made love.

"Okay," she said, starting to rise.

"Wait. Change of plans." He pulled her back down. "Here seems like a good place."

"In the living room?" That surprised her. He had definite ideas about things. Sex on the sofa didn't fit in with what she knew about him.

"On the floor. I want you now." He hadn't needed to say the words, since his face was flushed and the bulge in his sweatpants was growing larger. "Stand up and strip."

"Is that an order?" She raised her eyebrows in question, pretending to be shocked, but desire formed low in her belly.

"Yes." He rose and shucked out of his clothes with amazing speed.

So that was how this was going to be, she thought. Two could play this game. She, too, yanked off her clothes and put her hands on her hips, eyeing him. He was definitely ready. His arousal thrust out toward her. "Now what?"

"Take me in your mouth." His gaze challenged her. He had to know that she wouldn't deny him, and she knew what he liked. They'd had a few nearly sleepless nights during which she'd figured that out, but those had been in bed… except the memorable episode in the shower. He wanted something a little different from her this time.

Okay, she could do different. She grabbed a sofa pillow and tossed it to the floor at his feet before dropping to her knees. Placing her fingers at his ankles, she slowly worked her hands up his legs, feeling his muscle and strength. He stood motionless, but when she glanced up, his eyes were focused on her every move.

Her hands went to his butt, fingers gripping tightly. Only then did she touch her lips to his dick. He moaned but remained still as she swirled her tongue around the tip. She took more of him in her mouth, savoring his hard length and listening for any sounds he made. He was being stoic, confining himself to just that one moan, but she wanted to make him give more. She sucked hard, taking him in deep, and felt elated when he gasped and pushed against her. Oh, yeah. She was having an effect on him. If he wanted physical, she could give him that. She repeated the action, this time scraping her teeth lightly along his dick.

"Jesus," he muttered. "A man can't take much of that."

"Giving up so soon?" She smiled up at him and languidly stretched out on the floor at his feet. His eyes were on her, making heat rise inside her. "Are you just going to look, or..." She touched her own nipple as she spoke, knowing that was a turn-on for him. He was on the floor with her instantly, his mouth going to where her fingers had been.

"I want you so much," he said as he moved to her other breast. His hands were roaming over her stomach and the tops of her thighs, pulling sensation and desire from every inch of her. And she wanted him too, more than she should.

It wasn't long before he'd slipped on a condom and was straddling her, separating her legs with his own. He paused then, seeming to take in every inch of her, almost as though he were trying to memorize her body. She couldn't quite read his mood, and the moment was gone too quickly for her to understand what he was feeling.

And then he was inside her, moving with a pounding rhythm that drove them up and up. She tightened her legs around him and tilted her body up while her hands dug into the muscles of his back. The most intense orgasm of her life rocked through her. She cried out his name before his mouth covered hers in a searing kiss as his abdominal muscles contracted and she felt the magnitude of his release.

He rolled off and lay next to her, his body not quite touching hers as their breathing returned to normal. She wanted to be held, to curl into him, but that didn't feel right, so she stayed where she was, unsure of what was happening between them.

Suddenly, he pushed to his feet and reached for his pants. "I need to check the security system. I'll see you upstairs, okay?"

He didn't wait for an answer before leaving the room. As she struggled to a sitting position and found her shirt, she wanted to say that it wasn't okay. She wasn't okay. Sure, she was satisfied six ways to Sunday, but she also felt like she'd been thrust aside.

Her connection with Kenton seemed more tenuous, not stronger like it should after such an intimate encounter.

14

———

Two mornings later, when Mia's alarm sounded, Kenton's arm came across her body. He was sleepy and warm, softer than he often was, and she liked that. In bed, at least, he was focused entirely on her. Other times, his attention was distracted by their situation, which she found frustrating, even dismissive.

"No need to go," he said in her ear.

"Work," she whispered back groggily. "Doughnuts don't make themselves."

The truth was that she was looking forward to getting out of the house for her shift, hoping the normalcy of work would reduce her stress levels. The entire household had spent the day before on high alert, with Kenton getting edgy each time she or one of the girls even approached a window or door. It was no way to live.

"They do today." He tightened his hold on her. "You're not going."

"Who's going to stop me? You?" She smacked him lightly on the shoulder, thinking he was kidding.

"Mia," he said, his tone serious. "I talked to your boss last night. You're on a leave of absence."

"Excuse me?" She rolled away from him and turned on a bedside light.

"It's not safe for you to go to the bakery," he explained, make that decreed, "and I can't be there to protect you *and* here for the girls."

"So you made the decision for me." A flicker of guilt passed over his expression, but it didn't last. He didn't feel bad about this. Not really. "I can't believe you did that. I like working at the bakery."

"I know, and you can go back as soon as this mess is cleared up. I had the owner's word on it." He tried to reach for her, but she evaded him and got out of bed. Unwilling to fight with him while naked, she grabbed her robe and cinched it tightly around her.

"You could have told me this last night. Why didn't you?" she demanded. His lips pinched together, and he looked away. Ha! He hadn't wanted her to be upset with him. Well, too bad. "I'm taking a shower, and I'm locking the bathroom door."

She stormed into the bathroom and took a long, hot shower, letting the streams of water absorb her tears of frustration. Oh, she understood why she couldn't go to work. She wasn't foolish. Anyone could walk in the back door of the bakery at any time. But did Kenton have to be so dictatorial about it? Couldn't they have had a conversation at some other time than four in the morning?

When she went back in the bedroom, he was gone, so she sat down on the edge of the bed. She was going to have to play by the rules he established until the situation was over, and then… she couldn't think about that just yet.

She went to the kitchen, started a pot of coffee, and began pulling ingredients from cabinets. If she couldn't bake at work, she could do it here. By the time Kenton brought the twins to breakfast, she had chocolate chunk and lemon poppyseed muffins ready for them and had baked herself into a better frame of mind.

While she cut muffins into quarters and buttered them, Kenton settled the girls in their chairs and got them cups of milk.

"Are you hungry?" she asked him. He was sweaty, so she assumed he'd worked out in the basement, where he had a home gym.

"If you have extra." He was feeling out her mood.

She gestured to the muffins cooling on the counter. "Help yourself."

"Mia, I'm really sorry, but…"

"I know." She held up a hand. "It was the only option. But please don't forget that I'm an adult, too, and deserve to be consulted." Those were the words that had stayed with her while baking the muffins. Now that they were out, her anger diminished.

"Won't happen again," he said, as he grabbed three muffins from the counter and put them on a plate.

She didn't see how it could happen again, but she accepted his apology for what it was. If she wasn't working, she was going to have to keep herself very busy around the house, and that meant more time in the kitchen. "I bake when I'm stressed. What's your favorite dessert?"

He hesitated, no doubt unsure of the sincerity of her offer. "Always been a fan of a good pie."

"All right. A pie it is. I have some cherries in the freezer. What else is in the plans for the day?" She was hoping he'd spend some time with the girls. The day before, he'd been absorbed in meetings and whatnot and had only seen them briefly. In the short time they'd all lived together, the twins had grown used to having his attention, which meant they asked for him often. She'd had to make excuses for him yesterday.

"I have a meeting with my team in an hour," he said, "and when the kids are down for their nap, I want to show you some defensive moves."

She squinted at him. Did he honestly expect her to need those? Apparently he did. His face was deadly serious and his jaw set. Well, okay, it wouldn't hurt her to know something about self-defense. She'd taken a course years ago, so a refresher was probably a good idea. She nodded her agreement and turned her attention to the girls. When she glanced back, he was gone.

Throughout the morning, she loosely followed the schedule that Kenton had established for the twins, turning baking the pie into a morning lesson for the girls on how to measure ingredients. She had to admit following a plan did make the day go more smoothly. Not that she was dismissing her free-range parenting ideas altogether. Kids needed choice. She simply adjusted what they had choices over. By afternoon, the girls were tired and happy to take their afternoon naps. Once they were down, she sought out Kenton in his office.

"I'm ready for training," she announced as she entered. His laptop was open, showing small images of several security cameras in various rooms of the house. "I didn't know you had all that." She'd known there was a system but hadn't realized the extent.

"I've expanded it," he said. "Added sensors to all doors and windows and changed the settings so the footage records."

"Very sophisticated," she commented, thinking that sometimes she forgot to lock her car. What would he think of that? "I'm sure it will keep us safe."

He scrubbed a hand over his face. "Not as much as I'd like us to be. I'm seriously considering returning to North Africa to finish the mission I failed on."

She was shocked by his announcement. Traveling halfway around the world seemed an extreme response to their situation.

"Can you do that?" She didn't know how Special Forces worked, but she didn't think he could just fly off to Africa because he wanted to.

"I'd have to get permission from my CO to join the SEAL team that's already in place," he admitted. "But I think he'd grant it."

"Is that wise?" She was still reeling from his suggestion. "I mean, you could be hurt or…"

His steady gaze met hers, and she knew she'd said the wrong thing. "I know how to handle myself on a mission, Mia. It's what I do for a living, you know."

"I didn't mean it that way." She really hadn't. He seemed so invincible, and despite her anger at him earlier, she was afraid for him. And herself and the girls. Afraid of what might happen to them if he left. "But I'd worry about you. And aren't you needed here?"

"That's what's stopped me from asking my CO. I don't want to leave you and the girls under the protection of someone else. I made this mess, and it's up to me to see it through." His eyes strayed to the laptop screen where the image of the twins sleeping was displayed. "My actions have never put anyone else in danger before. Not like this."

Mia couldn't listen to him beat himself up anymore, so she reached out, setting her hand on his shoulder, unsure if he'd accept her touch or bat it away. When he didn't rebuff her, she mirrored the touch with her other hand and moved between him and his desk. "I'd be frightened here without you. I'm not going to lie about that. I know you trust your buddies, but it wouldn't be the same."

He'd introduced Patrick and Anderson to her yesterday, and she knew that they and another man were taking shifts watching the house. It was a comfort, but it wasn't the same as having Kenton close. Plus, she had her own selfish reasons for not wanting Kenton to put himself in danger. She cared for him. They had no future as a couple, she got that, but knowing it didn't change how she felt.

He let out a long sigh and rested his hands on her hips. "I'll stay. It just… grates on me." She bent closer and kissed him lightly.

"Come on," she said, drawing back. "Let's hit the gym while the girls are sleeping."

He led her to the basement, where he had a mat already spread on the concrete floor. Over the next hour, he showed her several ways to break an assailant's hold, whether she was approached from the front or behind. He made her practice the moves over and over. She didn't know how effective her actions would be against a trained mercenary, but she tried her best to learn the techniques. Throughout it, Kenton treated her like a student, not a lover. That felt odd and unsettling.

At the end of the session, he retreated to his office and left her to deal with the girls. She recognized that they were her nieces to raise, but having him as a sort of co-parent lately had made the awesome weight of her responsibilities seem lighter.

Not meant to last, she told herself, as she headed to the girls' room. Partway up the stairs, she got a call from her apartment complex's office. She paused to listen to the rental agent. The refurbishment of her apartment was ahead of schedule, and she would be able to move back in as early as the following week. Good news, of course, and Mia thanked the lady on the phone. The question was, would she be able to move out of Kenton's home so soon?

She hesitated with her hand on the doorknob, trying to get her emotions in check. Part of her was desperate to move on and be free of the threat that hung over their heads. But part of her would miss being here, would miss Kenton.

15

"All better," Mia said as she kissed Emma's boo-boo and put on a Band-Aid. They'd been in the backyard having a scavenger hunt when the girl took a tumble and skinned her knee. Mia had brought them both inside so she could patch up the injury.

Like her, the girls had been reluctant to go in, since it was the only outside time they were allowed. Kenton had kept them locked down for the past several days, to the point where Mia was just about ready to barge out the door and make a break for her car. Kenton wouldn't even allow her to go to the grocery store. He'd had food delivered based on a list she provided. This was no way to live.

"Hungry," Ava said with a tug on Mia's sweatshirt.

Without thinking, Mia consulted the clock. Morning snack time was still five minutes away. She caught herself before saying that, because what difference did it make if they ate a tiny bit ahead of schedule? She'd been adjusting to the more rigid schedule that Kenton imposed, and even liked parts of it, but enough was enough.

"What would you like?" she asked Ava with a smile.

"Cookie," Ava answered.

"Nice try, kiddo, but we have to eat something healthy. How about apple slices instead? And then maybe a small cookie," Mia said.

She got the girls settled at the table and sliced up an apple into bite-sized chunks suitable for toddlers. Mia had learned so much about raising children in the time she'd had guardianship of her nieces. At first she had just been trying to make it all work. But now she was feeling more comfortable with that aspect of her life. Maybe it was the structure that Kenton felt was necessary; maybe it was just the motherlike figure she was becoming. Either way, it felt good, which was a blessing, considering the threat against them. It was important that *something* felt good.

Outside, she heard the mower start. Much of the lawn was already covered in leaves from the two large maple trees in the backyard. She didn't see why the grass needed to be cut, but if it kept Kenton's mind occupied, it was fine with her. He'd been on edge, unwilling to play with the girls and willing to snap at her. The previous evening had been spent in silence, and at bedtime, she'd retreated to the guest room that she'd used when she first moved in. She missed his warmth and strength wrapped around her, but a distance was growing between them. Silence had continued at breakfast, and she felt her nerves were stretched thin. She was tired of trying to dance around his ill humor.

"Done with your snacks, girls?" she asked, keeping her tone light. They'd eaten their apples and an oatmeal raisin cookie each. "Let's take our coloring books to the back deck. The sunshine is so beautiful today."

Mia gathered up the crayons and books and got the girls situated on the deck. When she sat down next to them, she turned her face upward, enjoying the warmth on her skin. Autumn was coming on fast, but days like this reminded her of all the beauty of the season.

"I want blue," Emma said, bringing Mia's attention back to the girls. Emma clutched the midnight blue crayon in her hand, holding it out of her sister's reach.

"We have to share. You use it for a minute, and then it'll be Ava's turn," Mia told the girl, who thankfully complied without a fight. With order restored, Mia looked to where Kenton was mowing toward the rear of the property. "Oh, no," she said when she saw Kenton headed straight toward an old ball she'd left in the yard, mostly hidden under a clump of leaves. It was one of the items the girls had been scavenging for. They'd gotten distracted from their game by Emma's skinned knee and hadn't retrieved the rest of the hidden toys.

She winced when he ran over the half-deflated ball and it got jammed in the underside of the mower, stopping it.

"What the hell?" he yelled as he flipped the mower over and saw the ball. "Son of a bitch."

Before he could swear any more, Mia sprinted across the lawn toward him, knowing the girls were safe on the deck.

"Kenton," she said, but he rounded on her before she could get anything else out.

"I've told you and the girls that cleaning up toys is important. Now look what's happened." His voice was raised, not quite yelling but close.

"Emma hurt herself, so we went in without picking things up," she said, trying to explain. "It's just an old ball."

"I'm not worried about the damn ball." He kicked at the mower. "The mower's jammed, and I've got the rest of the yard to do yet. This'll put me off my schedule for the day."

She held her peace for a moment, knowing that his reaction was about more than the toy. It was about the horrible situation imprisoning them.

"It's not that big a deal," she said, trying to reason with him. "The important thing is—"

"Save it," he said. "I don't want your excuses."

"What is that supposed to mean?" Her hands went to her hips. "My excuses?"

"You make excuses for why the girls don't do well. If they have an accident, you blame it on something other than them."

"They're children. Young children," she argued, her temper rising. "And you know what? They are mine. I'm their guardian, and I'm sick of your trying to dictate and control what we do. I'm leaving."

"You can't leave," he said flatly.

She knew his blunt statement was no more than the truth. She couldn't leave because her apartment wasn't ready yet, but she'd be damned if she was going to stay here and listen to him snarl at her. "I may not have anywhere to go, but I can at least take the girls for a walk while you cool off."

"Don't." His voice was full of warning.

She turned away from him and walked rapidly back toward the girls. "Come on, girls, we're going to take a little stroll around the block before lunch. Maybe we can collect different kinds of leaves while we go."

The girls, excited about some freedom, both hopped up and took her hands. Rather than going through the house, Mia led them out a gate and headed for the front sidewalk. She was so done with the forced confinement and done with Kenton, too.

She glanced back as she closed the gate and saw him standing where she'd left him. His eyes were focused on her, but his expression was almost sheepish. Did he feel bad about jumping down her throat? He might, but that wouldn't prevent her from taking her walk.

"This way, girls." She kept their hands held tightly in hers as they walked. By the time they reached the first corner, each girl had picked up leaves in their free hands. "That's a sycamore leaf. Look what a pretty shade of yellow that one is." She kept up a dialogue with the girls. This was what it should be like, she thought. She should be taking nature walks with them and encouraging them to respect the world around them, not hiding from it as they had been doing.

"Mia." Kenton's voice boomed down the quiet street, but she didn't bother to turn around. She couldn't deal with him right now. "Mia, on your left!"

She spun her head in that direction and saw a white van speeding toward her from the cross street. Oh, god. She froze for a second and was just leaping into action when the van squealed to a stop at the curb next to her. The side door opened and three men launched out, headed for her and the girls. Before she could react, one man grabbed Ava and another snatched Emma away. The last assailant went for Mia, taking hold of her arms. She broke his grasp using one of the techniques Kenton had taught her. As she whirled around to try to rescue the girls, Kenton charged in with Anderson, who'd been on patrol outside the house.

"Get back," Kenton yelled to her.

Everything after that happened lightning fast. Kenton and Anderson subdued the men who had taken the girls and set the girls free. They raced toward her on their short legs, and she opened her arms to them, lifting them both and backing away as fast as she could. She sat on the steps of a nearby house and held them, keeping their little faces against her so they didn't see the conflict that ensued. She couldn't take her eyes off it.

Kenton and Anderson yanked the driver and another man out of the van, tossing them on the grass beside their companions. She watched as Kenton lifted one man roughly by his shirt and spoke to him. Even though she couldn't hear the words, she saw Kenton's fierce expression and the man's belligerence. He worked his way down the line, questioning each man. She clutched the girls closer, thankful that Kenton and Anderson had been watching out for them… and ashamed that she'd put the girls in danger by taking them for a walk.

Soon, police cars pulled up and officers took the men into custody.

Kenton approached her then. "Take the girls back to the house," he said. "I'm going to be a while cleaning this up."

"Is… is there anything I can do?" she asked. Part of her wanted to apologize to him, but she couldn't find the words, not when he was looking like a warrior.

"Just keep them safe," he said and was gone.

It was hours later when he returned home, and the twins were sound asleep. Bedtime had been rough, as they worked through the trauma of being grabbed by unknown men. That had brought back Ava's ordeal at the festival, and the girls had sobbed until they were too tired to keep their eyes open.

After she was sure they wouldn't wake again, Mia had made her way downstairs and started a fire in the hearth. There was something soothing about it that she needed. Maybe it was the memory of the evening when the power was out and the closeness she'd felt with Kenton then. She was sitting on the couch with Eliot curled up at her feet when she heard the front door open and close. A few seconds later, Kenton came into the living room, looking exhausted.

She immediately stood up and moved to close the distance between them. He stilled her with a dismissive wave. "Can I get you a beer or a glass of wine? Have you had dinner?" she asked.

"No, thanks," he said, dropping onto the couch. "Come sit with me." He held out a hand to her, and she hesitated only a second before joining him. He laced their fingers together and rested their joined hands on his thigh. His action seemed intimate, but she couldn't read the vibe he was putting off.

"We're safe," he said after a minute of silence. "The guys who attacked you today were guns for hire, but they led us back to who hired them. It was Ocampa, the leader of the child-trafficking ring I told you about. Surprisingly, after a little persuasion, one of them confessed to knowing where Ocampa is hiding out."

Mia didn't want to ask what "persuasion" meant exactly. "So it was what you thought? This was left over from your last mission."

"Yeah. I spoke with my CO. The SEALs have a tactical team in the area where Ocampa is hiding, so they'll be dispatched to bring him in."

"Will they be successful?" she asked. A hard stare was her only answer. Of course they would, the look said. "So it's over?" She wanted to be sure of this.

"Yep. No more threat." Eliot had risen to rest his head against Kenton's knee and beg for attention. Kenton ran his hand over the dog's head and stroked his ears.

Mia sat back, feeling relief and something more complicated than that. The threat had kept her at Kenton's house, had kept her and the girls close to him. She'd chafed against the restraint, especially during the past few days. Without the threat, she could resume her normal life. That was good, right?

So why did she feel hollow inside?

16

The next day Mia hung up the phone after the second of two very welcome calls. Both had brought good news. The first came early in the morning and had been a complete surprise. The bakery's owner was so pleased with her work that he was offering to bring her on full time. When she'd taken the job it had been for the summer season, from April to October. Staying at a position longer than six months was new for Mia, but the bakery suited her, so she gladly accepted the offer.

Then the apartment complex called and said she could move back in immediately. They even emailed her pictures of her redone place. Before the fire, the apartment had been adequate, nothing special or fancy. The rebuild had added windows for more light, and somehow, they'd reconfigured the floor plan to accommodate a second bathroom as well as a larger kitchen. The new setup would suit her needs so much better as the girls grew.

Now, with a permanent job and an all-new apartment, she was ready to resume the normal life that had been interrupted by the fire. To celebrate, she decided to make a special lunch for her and Kenton.

Kenton was busy throughout the morning and early afternoon with calls, not taking a break to eat, so when she got the girls down for their nap, she tapped lightly on his office door.

"Lunch, Kenton."

"Be right there," he said, so she walked back to the dining room by herself.

She'd set the table in the formal room, spreading a tablecloth on the shiny mahogany surface and using nicer plates and glasses that she'd found in a cabinet. The lunch was only salad and sandwiches, but she placed the food in pretty serving dishes and fussed with how everything was presented.

When she stood back and surveyed it all, the same hollow feeling from the evening before struck her. She was leaving, probably soon, but the thought didn't have the appeal it once had. Her apartment would be lovely, but she'd miss Kenton, even if he had been difficult lately. That had been the stress of the threat, so she was hoping things would be better now.

Dare she hope that they could be a family as, for a brief while, it had seemed like they were? The day of the drive and fall festival came back to her. The afternoon, before the attempted kidnapping, had been perfect. She'd fallen a little in love with Kenton that day. More in love, really, she admitted to herself. It had been coming on since the night of the power outage, when he'd kissed her so lovingly.

She sighed and sank into her chair. Was it too much of a leap to think he'd want to continue the life they'd had for the past weeks? Maybe over their luncheon she'd find the courage to ask him. The more she thought about it, the more she thought she could do that. He wanted a family. His mother had told her that, and why else would he own such a large home? So maybe it could work, and she and the girls would be his family. The thought sent a happy glow through her.

"Something special going on?" he asked, making her jump as he walked into the room.

"Several somethings," she said, giving him a smile. "I thought we deserved a celebration."

"Okay." He took the chair next to her and reached for the sandwich platter. "What for?"

"For starters, my apartment's ready for me and the girls to move back into." She watched him closely for anything that might suggest he didn't want them to go, but his face was carefully blank. Perhaps he was just being guarded since he didn't know how she felt, so she kept her tone cheerful. "They've improved the design, so it'll be better than ever."

"That's good," he said almost as if he hadn't heard her.

"And, of course, we're celebrating the end of the threat against us." She put as much enthusiasm into her voice as possible.

"Yeah, that." He took a bite of his sandwich. "The whole damn thing's been a shitshow from beginning to end. I just spent hours on a call debriefing from it."

She wanted to ask if the SEAL team had caught the man behind the attacks, but she was worried that he'd snap at her, so she said nothing. She wasn't getting through to him anyway.

"If only I could figure out where I went wrong with my planning," he said. Was he back to reliving his failed mission? "And why the intel was slow to catch up to the reality," he continued. He stabbed at the salad that he'd piled on his plate. "That bugs me. The incident at the fall festival should never have happened if I'd had better intel."

Mia sat back in her chair, trying to decide her best course of action. Talking about family seemed out of place now, and she was tired of listening to him blame himself and rehash the mission. It did no good.

"You can't make the past better by thinking about it. You have to move on and look at the positives," Mia said. She'd understood that long ago, when she was recovering from the grief of her parents' deaths.

"Right," he said, his tone sarcastic. "Some reflection would be a good thing for you."

"What do you mean?" She straightened, his words feeling like a slap across her face.

"If you thought about your actions more, past and future, you could do better with your nieces. They're only going to get more complicated as they get older, you know."

"I think I'm doing just fine." The girls were healthy and about as well-adjusted as children who had lost their parents at so young an age could be.

He gave her a you've-got-to-be-kidding look. "You don't even have a stable job. It's only seasonal work. You hadn't mentioned that detail to me. I learned it when I talked to the owner about you taking a leave of absence."

"Maybe it was none of your business." She hadn't intentionally kept that fact to herself. She just had felt no need to tell him, for the obvious reason that she'd get a different job when she needed to. No big deal. "Besides, I've always been able to find work."

He shook his head. "You may have been able to live that way when you were single, but not with the girls. Kids take planning and commitment," he concluded, slapping his hand down on the table. "And you have to have some personal goals. I mean, what kind of career do you want to have? You should finish your education and get a degree, the kind that gives you enough income to raise two kids."

"Thanks for your advice," she said, rising from the table. "But I'm not here to have my life planned for the next five years." She shoved her chair in as she spoke. "And maybe, just maybe *you* would do better to let things go, to not torture yourself with the past. Move on, move forward, and take things as they come. People might even like you more if you weren't so uptight."

Kenton's face hardened, and his body went rigid. She'd said more than she should have, but her anger and frustration had boiled over. But she had to finish this conversation. "I have just two more things to say to you. One, the bakery called this morning, and they're taking me on full time, year-round." She managed not to vocalize the *so there* she wanted to add. "And two, the girls and I are moving out today. I'll pack what's necessary and come back for the rest another time."

She left the nearly untouched lunch on her plate, striding past him on her way to the stairs. Part of her wanted to burst into tears. That was the biggest confrontation she'd ever had with anyone in her life. It left her shaking, but that was nothing compared to the sense of loss that hit her as she walked into the girls' room. Any hope she'd had for a life with Kenton was completely dashed.

Fine, she thought, grabbing a bag and starting to stuff it with clothes. She was fine on her own. She didn't need him and his dictatorial ways. She sucked in a breath. But, god, it had been nice for a while to be with him.

17

"Christ, who now?" Kenton muttered when he heard his front doorbell ring. Since he was at his desk, he brought up the security camera feed and saw his mother standing on his porch with a shopping bag in her hands. He groaned. He loved his mom, but he wasn't in the mood for company.

It had been a hellish two days. He was on edge because the SEAL team in North Africa had failed to apprehend Ocampa, and Mia had left with the girls. He shouldn't miss them as much as he did, but he'd damn near shed a tear when he'd found a zip bag of training pants that he'd stashed in his office in case of emergency. On top of that, the playhouse he'd ordered for them as a surprise had shown up that morning. He could hardly look at the box's image of happy kids climbing on brightly colored plastic. He'd stashed it in the garage unopened.

He'd give it to Mia eventually, for the kids, but he wasn't ready to see any of them. He couldn't be in control of himself in Mia's presence yet. He had so botched that last conversation with her. She'd made him lunch and wanted to talk about her job and apartment, and he'd been nothing but negative. And self-centered. That's what bothered him the most. She'd been reaching out to him, and he'd ignored her feelings. Hell, he'd belittled her. He didn't think he'd ever done that to a human being before. Why he did it to her, he couldn't say.

The damn bell sounded again. Shit. He made his way toward the front door, knowing that his mother wasn't going to give up and go away. She'd have seen his truck in the driveway and know he was home.

"Hi, Mom," he said as he opened the door.

"Hello, honey." She ran a hand over his cheek. "You really should shave off this scruff."

"I like it." They'd had this same conversation a million times. "What brings you over?" He'd texted her yesterday to accept an upcoming dinner invitation because he'd known he wasn't going to be able to put off seeing her much longer. Her visit today, though, was a surprise.

"I brought some toys for the girls. Where are they?" She was looking around his entryway. Until two days ago, the girls' sweatshirts had hung on pegs near the door.

"They moved out. Mia's apartment was ready ahead of schedule." He hadn't mentioned that in his text.

"Oh," His mom put the shopping bag on the floor. "I'm sorry to hear that." She looked disappointed. What the hell was that about?

"Why?" he asked, going for a half-joking tone. "I'm not enough for you anymore?" He knew he was attempting to use humor to avoid thinking about his feelings and explaining them to his mother. He didn't want to think about how empty his house felt.

"Of course you are, but…"

"I'll get to work on getting you grandkids soon, I promise. It's in my five-year plan." House, wife, kids. That had been his mantra. One had to follow the others in an orderly pattern.

"It seemed that you had a perfectly lovely family already started," his mom said.

"Mine? They weren't my family," he said. Mia had made that very clear when she walked out.

"And why not? Mia's a beautiful woman who's also fun. The girls are adorable, and I thought you liked them." His mother's face was full of disappointment.

"I did. I do," he stammered.

"So why not keep the family that landed in your lap and work on something else for the next five years?" His mother pinned him with the same look that she'd used to interrogate him when he was five and stole an extra cookie from the jar.

"Because I have a plan, Mom. I would think you of all people would understand that." He didn't say what came to his mind first, which was that Mia and the girls weren't his. They never had been, and that was just as well.

"What does that mean?" She turned away from him and walked into his living room. "Too quiet in here," she observed before sitting down. "Now, explain what you just said."

He followed her, since he wasn't going to get out of this conversation. "Well, you get it. You've been a planner since I was a little kid. We had a family calendar, remember? Every soccer practice, scout meeting, and dentist appointment was carefully documented."

"Sure," she readily agreed, "parents need an organizational system or it's chaos, but that was a daily or weekly schedule. That wasn't life."

"It sure as hell looked like it. You were regimented. I didn't have an issue with the rigid rules in the Navy because I'd grown up with you. Breakfast at seven, dinner at six. No snacks. Bedtime based on age. Precisely one hour of TV per day. You should have been the captain of a ship."

"Is that how you saw it?" his mother said softly, her disappointed expression shifting to hurt.

"How could I see it any other way? Do you remember when Uncle Ned came home after failing in Nashville? You used him as an example of what not to do. I was twelve, and I took it to heart." Before that, he'd harbored a secret desire to just take off on a trip with no destination. Go and not worry about where he was going to spend the night or what places he'd visit. He'd pictured doing that after he graduated from high school. He'd enjoy complete freedom, at least for a time. But that dream had died when his parents made it clear that taking chances and trusting in fate was a mistake, and he'd switched his attention to the creation of a master plan for his life.

"God, I'm sorry about that." His mother seemed truly stricken. "It wasn't Ned's first time attempting something like that, and I was frustrated with his unwillingness to… play by the rules of society."

"Wait," Kenton said. "What are you saying?"

"Oh, sweetie. You're right, to a point. I did try to play by the rules. I read all the parenting books and listened to people's advice, and you know what I discovered? They contradicted each other. Dreadfully, at times. No two books ever agreed on how to handle a problem. When you were little, I was lost, and your father decided we needed a system. You know how he is."

Trent Fitzpatrick was an electrical engineer. He never tackled anything without a clear plan and a schematic on paper. Kenton was beginning to wonder if he'd misunderstood his parents completely. Maybe all kids did.

"What we learned, though, was that no answer ever worked all the time. We had to use our instincts to decide what the right path was. And maybe we erred too much on the side of caution by exerting so much control over everything, but we only did so because we knew control wasn't truly possible. We were faking it half the time. Am I making any sense?"

"Yeah," he said. Before he found Mia and the girls living in his home, he wouldn't have understood this conversation. Like his parents, he wanted to give the appearance of having everything under control. He might be able to do that in his life as a SEAL, but raising a family was different.

A family. The family he wanted. For the first time, Kenton let himself feel the emotions that he'd been doggedly storing away, and he recognized that they weren't a box he could put in the back of the garage. He missed Mia and the girls with all his heart, but they were gone from his life.

He dropped into a chair and buried his head in his hands. He was such an ass. He hadn't even helped her move out. She'd texted to let him know she was picking up the rest of her stuff after work, and he'd made sure not to be there, which meant she'd had to lug the girls' cribs and all their toys and clothes by herself. Was that forgivable? Was the way he'd acted for the past several days forgivable? Shit, he didn't know.

"Is there a book on how to tell someone you're sorry?" he finally asked after a long silence.

"Probably a thousand, and none of them are any good," his mother said. "All you have to do is speak from your heart. That's what will matter."

"Mom, can you let yourself out?" Kenton got to his feet, knowing what he needed to do. He didn't know how to do it, but he'd figure it out, use his instincts. Hopefully, they'd guide him right when he was standing in front of Mia.

"Sure. I'll leave these toys in the girls' room." She lifted the shopping bag.

He grabbed his truck keys, hoping his mother's confidence wasn't misplaced. He was running down the porch steps when Patrick's ringtone sounded from his phone.

"Hey, buddy. I can't talk right now—"

"Get to Mia's apartment building pronto." Patrick's voice was calm but insistent. "We've got trouble. I'll meet you there."

18

Mia wandered her redone apartment while the girls were playing in their bedroom. She liked everything she saw, from the pearly white walls and laminate flooring to the shiny new kitchen. It was all so much better than she'd expected. Her neighbors in the building felt the same way. She'd spoken with her fellow residents in the stairwell while she'd moved her things up the afternoon before.

Fortunately, Shasta had offered to help her when the bakery closed for the day. Together, they'd gotten everything from Kenton's house and placed it in the apartment before picking up the girls from day care. Since he hadn't been home, she'd slipped her house key under the mat by the front door and texted him to let him know she was out. It was an impersonal way to say goodbye to someone who had become so important to her, but she didn't see she had a choice.

Even though she'd stormed out of his house, her anger hadn't lasted long. Not past the drive to her apartment. Now all she had left was the hurt. Despite their argument, he was special to her, probably the best man she'd ever known. But she'd seen their relationship differently than he had. He couldn't picture them beyond the short term, since it wasn't in his plan. She could see the potential for their happiness, but it wasn't meant to be.

"I'm okay," she whispered to herself while standing in her kitchen. "I've got Ava and Emma to love, and that's all that matters." She had to remember that. Her little family was the only important thing. If Kenton didn't want them, that was his choice. She shook her head. She just didn't know how he could shut his heart off like that. Maybe he didn't love her, but the girls? Who could not love them? And he had seemed to when he took care of them. Maybe he'd been overly dedicated to his routines, but he'd taken the time to get to know both girls while they'd lived in his home.

"Aunt Mia," the two girls chorused, "come here."

When she got to their room, she found them both on the floor, coloring on the same large sheet of paper. Coloring at this age wasn't about staying in the lines. Large blobs of color in random shapes covered the paper.

"What's this? A decoration for your room?" Most of her decor had been lost in the fire, and she hadn't yet replaced it. She wanted to take the girls to the store and allow them to select pictures and curtains they liked.

"It's for Kenton," Emma announced. "Put his name on it."

How had the girls known she was thinking about him? And how much did he mean to them? It broke her heart.

"If you're asking me, you should say, 'Will you please put his name on it?'" She waited, and Emma dutifully repeated the phrase. Mia knelt on the floor and selected the red crayon. Along the top edge, she wrote "Kenton" in blocky print.

"Add a heart," Ava said, her voice soft.

"Sure." Mia gave her niece a smile.

"One for me, too." Emma pointed to where she wanted hers.

Mia felt tears gather in her eyes, but she placed the hearts where they asked. The images on the paper were unrecognizable, but the girls' sentiment was priceless. Mia would have to get it to him somehow, and the thought made her shaky. Could she face him?

"Is it all done now?" she asked, and they both nodded. "Clean up your crayons, then. How about you watch a movie while I make dinner?"

Both girls hopped up at the offer of a rare treat. She kept screen time very limited. Since the only television hooked up was in her bedroom, she let them climb onto her bed and lounge against the pillows, which was another treat. She started a princess movie for them, then headed back to the kitchen and put a pot of water on the stove for pasta.

While she waited for the water to boil, Mia pulled out her phone to make two calls, ones that she wouldn't let herself put off. She wanted to speak with Patrick and Anderson and express her gratitude for helping to protect her and the girls. She got through to both of them on the first try. They were good men. A lot like Kenton, but more relaxed about life. She thanked them, and they politely asked how she and the girls were, but neither made any mention of Kenton. And she couldn't bring herself to ask if they'd spoken to him.

She'd been hoping the gesture would give her closure, but it didn't work that way. Talking to Kenton's friends only made her miss him more, made the pain of being away from him stab deeper.

Everything did, if she was honest with herself. When she tried to choose the best drawer for her silverware, she thought that Kenton would analyze the configuration of the kitchen before making the decision. The same was true when she moved on to the spice rack. He probably would have put the bottles in alphabetical order so each one was easy to locate.

She drained the pasta, added three kinds of cheese, and put the mixture in the oven to bake. The girls loved homemade mac and cheese, and she wanted their first memories of the "new" apartment to be good ones. While she waited for dinner to cook, she continued to work her way through the purchases she'd made earlier in the day to restock the kitchen supplies. With two minutes left on the oven timer, she put the last items away.

There, her kitchen was set up. Her apartment was taking shape. She blew out a sigh, thinking she should have a sense of satisfaction, even happiness. But she didn't.

"I've got this," she said, trying to give herself a pep talk. "No reason to be upset." Inside, she wondered when she'd stop missing Kenton quite so much.

The timer beeped, and she put the macaroni and cheese on the counter to cool a little. She was setting the table when a knock sounded on her door. Hope flooded her. Maybe the universe was sending her Kenton.

Without looking through the peephole, Mia opened the door and felt the smile on her face freeze. Three men shoved their way into her apartment, the lead one immediately clamping a hand over her mouth to prevent her from screaming.

"Yell for help," a low voice threatened, "and I shall cut you first and then start on your nieces." He showed her the switchblade he held in his other hand. His tone of voice alone would have convinced her to comply. She nodded, and the pressure on her mouth relented.

"Mia Kingston." The man who had come through the door last spoke, and Mia shifted her eyes to him. He was clearly in charge, dressed better than the others, and there was something inherently dangerous about him. Perhaps it was his narrow, hawklike face or the sneer on his lips, but it gave her shivers.

"Who are you?" she asked, her voice trembling slightly.

"Let us sit," the man commanded. "I want to explain to you what is going to happen to you and your nieces."

The man who held her shoved her toward the couch. While she was moving, she slipped her hand into her hoodie's pocket. Anderson was the last person she'd spoken to, making his number her most recent contact. She tapped the screen, hoping she was hitting the send button. Perhaps he'd pick up and hear what was going on. It was the only thing she could think to do.

She could hear the movie playing in her bedroom and knew it was getting close to the final scene. The girls would seek her out when it ended. These men knew the girls were in the apartment, but she wanted to spare them as long as she could.

"Who are you?" she repeated. "Why did you burst into my apartment?" She tried to make her words clear, praying that Anderson was listening.

"My name is Marcus Ocampa," the man said with a certain level of pride in his voice.

Her breath hitched. She recognized that name. He was the man Kenton had failed to capture on his last SEAL mission.

"I see you've heard of me." Ocampa smiled, seemingly pleased.

"Yes," she was forced to admit, since she hadn't controlled her response. "You're infamous."

"Only among a small circle. Not many know my name. I believe Kenton Fitzpatrick must have told you about me."

"A little," she admitted.

"You are quite friendly with him." The word "friendly" had never sounded so sleazy.

"Not really." She forced herself to give a casual shrug. "We stayed at his house when we had nowhere else to go. That's my only connection to him."

"You lie so prettily." The smile stayed on Ocampa's thin lips. "You were his lover. Perhaps you still are. And he cared for your nieces as if they were his own. There is much more of a connection than you say."

"If that were true," she said, "I'd still be living with him."

"A lovers' spat?" This time she controlled her reaction to Ocampa's suggestion. "No matter. He'll figure out how much you mean to him when you're missing."

"Missing?" she repeated.

"Fitzpatrick led the team that crippled my enterprise and sent me into hiding. Making you and your little nieces go missing is my way of… how shall I say it? Taking revenge. Letting him know that I am better than he."

"What will you do with us?" she asked to keep him talking. The two men with Ocampa exchanged a knowing look that chilled her.

"Sell you to the highest bidders, of course." Ocampa seemed to relish his words. "Identical twin girls are very valuable commodities in my business."

"You're disgusting," she declared, her fury making its way through her fear. Her mind was going in a thousand directions, trying to figure out how to defend herself and the girls. She still had the whistle Kenton had given her stuffed in her jeans pocket, but could she pull it out and blow it before they took it from her? And if she did, would anyone realize it was a call for help?

"Fitzpatrick's life will never be the same," Ocampa said, his smile becoming more smug. "He will forever wonder what has happened to you. It will drive him mad."

"He won't care," she said. "He didn't want us." The sad thing was that her statement was true. He didn't appear to want them. He'd made no effort to communicate with her, not even responding to her text about the key. But he would help her if she was in trouble. And, oh lord, was she in trouble now.

How long would Ocampa be willing to chat? Once he got them into a vehicle, there would be no chance of rescue. If Anderson wasn't hearing this conversation, how long would it be before anyone noticed they were gone? The neighbors were busy moving into their own apartments. When she didn't pick up Eliot from the groomer's later, the woman would wonder what happened to her, but how long would it be before the groomer reported her missing?

From the bedroom, Mia heard the final song of the princess movie. The girls would come to find her any second. She had to act now. That thought was in her head when her door burst open, slamming back against the wall. Kenton bolted through, knocking one of her captors to the ground with a punch to the throat. The other raised a gun, but Kenton never stopped moving. A shot went off, echoing loudly in the room.

She blinked hard at the sound. When her eyes focused again, Kenton was on the ground with the gunman. Was he shot? She leaped up, but Ocampa clamped a hand just below her elbow. Mia lifted her arm immediately, raising it high and twisting to break his grip as Kenton had shown her. When Ocampa came at her again, she kicked him hard on the inside of his knee, making his leg buckle.

She was moving backward, away from Ocampa, when Kenton stepped between them and smashed a punch into Ocampa's face. The man crumpled and went down, striking his head on the coffee table before hitting the floor.

Strong arms came around her again, but she knew it was Kenton. She let herself collapse against his chest. He was breathing hard, his heart beating rapidly, but all she cared about was being with him.

"Shit, Kenton," a voice said from behind her. "You could have left us something to do."

She lifted her head enough to see Patrick and Anderson. They each had a man pinned to the ground, and Ocampa lay still near her couch.

"Are you shot?" She ran her hands over Kenton, suddenly remembering the gun firing.

"The shot went into the ceiling," he said. "I'm fine."

"Aunt Mia!" A cry came from her bedroom.

"The girls!" Mia lurched away from Kenton and ran to her bedroom. The girls were huddled together on her bed. "It's okay." She joined them in the bed and hugged them tight to her. "Nothing's going to hurt you."

The bed shifted, and she realized Kenton was next to her. His arms went around the three of them, and he placed kisses on the girls' foreheads. When he was done, he looked up, meeting her eyes, and she didn't know what to say.

He was opening his mouth to speak when they heard police sirens approaching. With a nod, he went back to her living room, leaving her to cuddle with the girls.

19

"Thank you," Mia said to Margaret as she yanked a sweatshirt over Emma's head in the parking lot of her apartment building. The girls had calmed down remarkably quickly, probably due to Kenton's presence. They'd heard the shot but had been spared listening to Ocampa's words.

"Not a problem," Margaret assured her. "I love having company. I think we'll do some painting. Does that sound fun, girls?" She got nods from both of them.

"And thanks for picking up Eliot from the groomer, too. I'm asking so much of you. I'm sorry."

"Stop that talk." The older woman took Mia's hand. "I'm happy to help."

That had been true in the past. Margaret had freely given Mia assistance after the fire, but she felt bad about imposing again. Kenton hadn't given her much choice, though. He'd called his mother and made the arrangements after explaining to Mia that she would be tied up with interviews and such for the evening.

"Let me know if you want them to stay over at my house. I can arrange that lickety-split." Margaret helped Mia buckle the kids in the car. When they pulled away, Mia stood in the parking lot among the police cars and waved goodbye to the girls. She rubbed her hands on her arms, trying to make sense of what had happened, but it was too much to process.

"Ready?" Kenton was suddenly beside her. "We need to get to the police station. Ride with me."

Since he didn't give her much choice and she felt too shaky to drive anyway, she got in his truck. They were both silent on the way to the station located behind the courthouse in downtown Hartsville. Before they got out of the truck, he turned to her.

"Just tell them exactly what happened," he said. "They'll ask you what seems like the same questions over and over, but that's how this works. I'm sorry you have to go through it, Mia."

"It's okay. I'm just glad he's been captured." She waited with her hand on the door handle, hoping Kenton would say more, but he didn't, so she got out of the truck and followed him inside.

The next hours were as he'd said. Police detectives interviewed her, asking questions and taking statements. Every detail of the moments that she was with Ocampa had to be discussed at length. Fortunately, Anderson's phone had recorded much of it, but they would need her statement as well for court.

When that was done, they were taken to another room where they spoke with Kenton's CO over a secure video link. She responded to the same questions once again and listened to Kenton elaborate on his actions and knowledge. Anderson explained about receiving the call and alerting Patrick and Kenton.

The men seemed unfazed by it all. It must be routine for them, but Mia was exhausted. When her phone glowed with a message, she excused herself to check it since she appeared to be done. It was Margaret letting her know that the girls had eaten dinner, painted with watercolors, and were now asleep in her guest room. She was not to come claim them until the morning.

"Everything okay?" Kenton asked as he came from the interview room to join her in the hall.

"Seems to be. Your mom says the girls are fine and staying the night at her house. I owe her." Mia would have to bake something special for Kenton's parents.

"She won't expect anything from you," he said. He was standing close to her, and Mia wanted to press herself against him and get lost in his warm hug. But he was treating her with polite distance. "We can go now. I'll drive you home."

"Thanks," Mia said. She was done in. She'd had no idea that answering questions could be so tiring, and the emotional strain of being so near Kenton and not touching him was almost more than she could endure after the day she'd had.

They walked outside with Patrick and Anderson before splitting off to head for Kenton's truck. An autumn chill was in the air, and the sun had set, leaving just a glimmer of light in the western sky. The coolness refreshed her, helped her find a sense of calm in the chaos of the day, but she didn't like the idea of going back to her apartment alone.

But that's what would happen. Kenton would drop her off, say his final farewell, and head out of her life. This time, though, she would try to say the right words to him before getting out of his truck. She'd thank him for allowing her to live in his house and for his kindness to her nieces. For herself, there wouldn't be any words. She couldn't express what he meant to her, and it was best not to try. She would say thank you and goodbye.

Kenton drove in silence through the downtown streets. As they passed the bakery, she saw cutouts of pumpkins and orange lights decorating the front windows. Other businesses were the same, everyone ready for the change in season. When Main Street intersected with South Street, Kenton should have turned left, but he kept on going straight.

"Kenton?" she said softly. "That was my turn." Was he on autopilot and not thinking?

"Like I said, I'm taking you home." He didn't turn to look at her until he pulled into a parking space and shut off the engine. It was dim in the cab, but she could see his face. He looked serious, maybe even nervous, and she wondered what could be coming next.

When he reached for her hand, she hesitated a moment. They were over, weren't they? The mission was done, the bad guy captured, her apartment habitable again. There was no reason for them to be together. No material reason. And yet he seemed to want something from her.

She placed her hand in his large, warm one, and his fingers tightened around hers.

"I'm taking you home, because you made the house I bought a home. It wasn't, before you came. It was beautiful, and I was proud to be its owner, but you… you made me want to walk through the door. You and the girls brought the house to life. Without you, it's just a house."

She bit her lower lip, trying to control her emotions. Was he saying that he wanted her in his life?

"I love you, Mia, with all my heart," he continued, "and I don't want to be without you. Will you come home and be with me?"

"You mean for tonight?" she asked. Did he only want her in his bed, or was this something more?

"I mean for every night for the rest of my life." He gave her a tentative smile. "Did you hear me say that I love you?"

"I heard you, but, Kenton, what about your plans?" She didn't want to ask, but she had to. "The girls and I aren't part of those."

"To hell with the plans. I don't have to wait and plan for the perfect wife and family. They showed up in my house. It's not what I expected to have happen, but I couldn't wish for more. Stay with me, Mia." He put his other hand over where theirs were joined. "Marry me."

"What?" She felt off balance, as if the world had tipped on its side. Had he just asked her to marry him? "You want me to…"

"Marry me. Be my wife, my lover, my friend. Will you?"

"Yes," she said, because there was only one answer to that question when he was asking her.

He pulled her closer, meeting her partway for a kiss. It wasn't a long one, but it was special, different somehow. When they parted, his face was serious again. What now?

"Will it clip your wings too much to stay in one place?" he asked.

"I like having new experiences," she said. "Being spontaneous and having fun. I can still find a way to do that." She could live in the lovely Victorian home with him and still be who she was.

"Spontaneous and fun?" He started the truck's engine and pulled back onto the street. "We're alone tonight. Mom has the girls, right?"

She laughed. "What are you suggesting, Kenton?"

"It wouldn't be spontaneous if we decided in advance, but I think it's safe to say we're not going to get much sleep tonight."

She watched his profile as he drove, and his grin was obvious. "That I can live with."

They turned onto their street, and she let out a sigh as they pulled into the garage. This was going to be her home. By itself, the house was beautiful, but with Kenton and the girls, Mia's life would be magical.

"What's that?" she asked when the truck's headlights illuminated a box in the corner of the garage. "Is that a playhouse?"

"Yeah, one of those big plastic ones. I ordered it a week ago. I thought the girls would like it."

"They'll love it. Oh, Kenton, you…" She couldn't find the words to express how she felt. When they went into the house together, she no longer needed words. Only actions mattered as Kenton showed her how much he loved her.

20

Kenton peered out the window at his front yard. An early December snowfall covered the lawn, setting the stage for the Christmas decorations that he and Mia had shopped for. They'd wanted just the right items, a mix between fun for the girls and elegance that matched the home. After much shopping and discussion, they'd decided on white lights and fresh greenery with candy cane and lollipop decorations along the sidewalk that led to the front door.

"Out, out." His mother flapped her hands at him in a shooing motion. "You can't see the bride before the wedding. Take the girls to the church, and we'll be ten minutes behind you."

Since Mia had no family, his parents had stepped in to help with the event. And his mother had loved every minute of it. She'd gone with Mia to the bridal boutique, helped pick out the cake, and was now making everyone snap to attention.

"Okay, okay. Am I allowed to see the girls, then?" he teased.

"Of course. Ava, Emma," Margaret called, "come on downstairs." The twins appeared at the top of the steps in matching white dresses with red ribbons tied around their waists and red headbands in their hair. "Slowly now, so you don't trip. Oh, aren't you both adorable?"

Kenton smiled. His mother was relishing the role of grandmother, too. He hoped that was still true in ten days when he and Mia returned from their honeymoon. Secretly, he suspected that they'd have to wrestle the girls away from his parents.

His dad came from the living room, dressed in a dark suit. Kenton had considered choosing a suit as well, but Mia had insisted he wear his uniform. He was glad now that she had. It felt right.

"We'll get Mia there in time," his dad said while Margaret got the girls into coats. "Do you have the rings?"

Kenton patted his pocket and felt for the two gold bands tied together with a ribbon. "Got 'em."

"I won't see you again before the wedding, son. Remember to enjoy it."

"I will," Kenton promised and gave both his parents a hug before getting the girls in his truck. At the church, Shasta took charge of the twins, waiting with them until it was time for them to walk down the aisle as the flower girls.

"Ready?" Patrick asked him. Like him, Patrick and Anderson were in uniform. Kenton hadn't been able to decide which of his two closest buddies should be his best man. They'd finally gotten together one evening, had a beer, and flipped a coin. Patrick won the toss and would stand next to him, but Anderson was giving the speech at the reception.

"Think so." He felt nervous about the wedding but not about the marriage. That was going to be pure bliss, based on the past two months. It had been a busy time, but his house had come alive with little girls giggling and a beautiful woman wrapped around him at night. It had all gone by so quickly. He was hoping to slow things down on the honeymoon.

"Got the rings?" Patrick asked as they made their way to the front of the church.

Kenton laughed at that. "Does everybody ask that question?"

"Guess so." Patrick blew a kiss to his wife, daughter, and two-year-old son where they sat in the front pew.

Music was playing from the pipe organ in the balcony as everyone settled into their seats. When Anderson escorted Margaret to her seat, Kenton knew the wedding was about to begin. Soon, the song changed to the familiar tune of the "Wedding March," and he focused his eyes on Ava and Emma as they started down the aisle. Each carried a basket of red roses and holly leaves, and they looked quite proud of themselves as they stayed in step and smiled at everyone. The wedding guests were enraptured. In the past months, Emma had mellowed ever so slightly, and Ava had found her voice more. Both seemed to be finding their personality.

When they reached him, he bent down and gave each of them a kiss on the cheek before they took their seats alongside his mother. He straightened and spied Mia entering the church on his father's arm. God, she was gorgeous. Her dress was a grown-up version of what the girls wore. Yards of white fabric, and a red ribbon encircling her slender waist. The strapless design showed off her lovely, kissable shoulders. But the best part was the smile on her face when she reached him.

He took her arm, and his dad stepped back, and the rest was magical. When the ceremony was over and he got to kiss the bride, their guests erupted in applause, making them both laugh.

"Us, too." Emma tugged on his pant leg. "We want kisses."

He squatted next to the girls and gathered them to him. "I love you both," he said and gave them the kisses they demanded. Mia had tears in his eyes when he stood up. He leaned close to her to whisper in her ear. "I love you most."

"I love you most, too," she whispered back, "and that's a lot, because I love them like anything."

"Me, too," he said, and then they each took a girl by the hand and the four of them walked back down the aisle together to lead their guests to the reception.

Since Mia had insisted that the party be fun, not formal, there was a cupcake at every place setting. As she'd said, why wait for the cake to be cut? She'd also wanted lots of Christmas decorations to celebrate the season and the occasion. The reception hall was ornamented with sparkly white snowflakes, fresh greenery, and red ribbon.

Later in the evening, Kenton and Mia were on the dance floor when he noticed a hush fall over the room. He looked around at the smiling faces. His parents, Emma and Ava, Mia's friends from the bakery, his buddies, their wives, and their kids.

"I think they may want something," he said to Mia.

"They want us to kiss." She leaned back in his arms and pointed above her to a sprig of mistletoe tied with ribbon.

"Happy to oblige," he said, putting his arm behind her waist and dipping her backward in a dramatic, Hollywood-style kiss. He caught the surprise on her face before he kissed her and felt a little proud of himself.

"So spontaneous of you," she said when he righted her. "I'm impressed."

"I plan to spend the next week and a half impressing you with my spontaneity. When can we leave?" They'd danced, eaten cake, smiled excessively, and had their pictures taken. He wanted to be away with his bride.

"I think now's good. I'm ready to be alone with you, but you still haven't told me where we're going." She'd asked him repeatedly, especially when she was trying to pack for the trip. He'd only said that they would be going someplace warm.

"That's because I don't know." He confessed the secret that he'd been keeping from her.

"You didn't plan something?" Her eyes went wide when he shook his head.

"As a matter of fact, we're going to decide right now." He turned to Anderson and Patrick. "Bring out the map, please." His buddies produced a large map of the southeastern states and attached it to a corkboard wall. Kenton handed Mia two darts and held two himself.

"What am I supposed to do with these?" She rolled the darts between her fingers and eyed him.

He steered her to a spot ten feet in front of the map. The wedding guests formed a half circle behind them. "Throw the darts and see where they land."

"This is how we're going to pick our destinations. Works for me," she said and squinted at the map. "Here goes."

Her first dart hit Key Largo, Florida. Perfect. It should be warm and sunny there. The second dart stuck in St. Augustine. Even better: the oldest city in the US hosted a massive Christmas lights festival. Even though Kenton hadn't made definite plans, he'd naturally researched possibilities.

She nodded, seeming satisfied with her choices. "Your turn."

He gauged the relative distance between her two picks. Where else would fit well with those destinations? He wasn't planning, not really, but he also didn't want to spend the time driving. He had plenty of other ideas of how to spend their honeymoon. He threw his first dart, and it bull's-eyed into Savannah, Georgia, an elegant and romantic city and the perfect place to begin their trip. A route took shape in his head, but where to put his last dart?

He smiled at her. "Any preferences?"

"Can you hit what you aim for?" she asked, looking at the map again.

"Usually." And he might have spent some time practicing recently. Leaving things entirely to chance would never quite work for him.

"In that case…" She leaned closer and kissed him on the cheek. "I'll confess a secret passion for theme parks."

He grinned, her words making his final throw easy. His dart sailed through the air and stuck in Orlando.

Their wedding trip couldn't have worked out better even if he'd planned it. After kissing and hugging the girls, shaking hands, and thanking people for their well wishes, they walked to his truck, which was pulled up to the entrance of the reception hall.

"What the…" He stopped walking, bringing Mia to a standstill next to him. She burst into laughter at the sight. Someone had decorated his truck. He shot a look toward Anderson and Patrick, who were both cackling like hyenas. Streamers hung from the antenna and mirrors, hearts were drawn on the windows, and a Just Married sign hung on the tailgate.

Kenton smiled, remembering how much his friends and family loved him and he loved them. That's what the day had been all about.

"Are you ready to depart, Mrs. Fitzpatrick?" he asked Mia.

"I am," she said. After one last hug for the girls, he helped his bride into the truck, carefully tucking her dress in around her. When he was in the driver's seat, he felt a sense of freedom that he'd never experienced before. They were going on a road trip, the two of them, for a week of nothing but enjoyment.

Kenton honked his horn and pulled away. As they turned onto the street, he reached for Mia's hand. "I love you," he said, wrapping his fingers around hers. "I *plan* to say that often in the coming years."

"That's a plan I'm happy to agree with. Now, let's go have some fun."

END OF THE SEAL'S INSTANT FAMILY
HARTSVILLE'S SEAL HEROES BOOK THREE

PS: Do you love hot blooded SEALS? Turn the page for an exclusive free book offer and exclusive extracts from **The SEAL's Pregnant Roommate** and **Guarding The Single Mother**.

FREE BOOK OFFER

Read FIVE full-length romances by USA Today best-selling author Leslie North for FREE! Over 600+ pages of best-selling romance with hundreds of FIVE STAR REVIEWS!

<u>Sign-up to her mailing list and get your FREE books</u>

THANK YOU!

Thank you so much for purchasing my book. It's hard for me to put into words how much I appreciate my readers. If you enjoyed this book, please remember to leave a review. Reviews are crucial for an author's success and I would greatly appreciate it if you took the time to review the book. I love hearing from you!

You can connect with me on:

MAKE AN AUTHOR'S DAY

There's nothing better than reading great reviews from readers like yourself, but there's more to it than simply putting a smile on my face. As an independent author, I don't have the financial might of a big NYC publishing house or the clout to get in Oprah's book club. What I do have, as my not-so-secret weapon is you, my awesome readers!

If you enjoyed this book, I'd be incredibly grateful if you could leave a quick review. No matter the length (short is fine!), your review will help this series get the exposure it needs to grow and make it into the hands of other awesome readers. Plus, reading your kind reviews is often the highlight of my day, so please be sure to let me know what you loved most about this book.

ABOUT LESLIE

Leslie North is the USA Today Bestselling pen name for a critically-acclaimed author of women's contemporary romance and fiction. The anonymity gives her the perfect opportunity to paint with her full artistic palette, especially in the romance and erotic fantasy genres.

Find your next Leslie North book visit LeslieNorthBooks.com or choose:

PS: Want sneak peeks, giveaways, ARC offers, fun extras and plenty of pictures of bad boys? Join my Facebook group, Leslie's Lovelies!

BLURB

Can these two lonely souls catch a lucky break in love?

Harley Von's never been lucky in life, let alone in love. And her streak of ill fortune continues when her long-lost brother passes away just as they were on the verge of reconnecting. On the run from a bad relationship, she's less than delighted to find herself sharing Sebastian's fixer-upper with his gruff but gorgeous friend, Garrett. With her ex breathing down her neck and a baby on the way, Harley's got plenty to deal with. Falling for a sexy SEAL isn't part of her plan.

Navy SEAL Garrett Moore isn't looking for romance. His life is the SEALs, end of discussion. Still, grieving and guilt-ridden over his teammate's death, he's determined to do what he can to help Sebastian's sister. And Harley's combination of vulnerability and determination is captivating. She's like a skittish fawn refusing to back down from a mountain lion.

He can't help feeling protective of her, especially when the ex shows up and gets physical. But Garrett's only in town for as long as it takes to repair the old house.

Love has a funny way of changing things, though

Grab your copy of
The SEAL's Pregnant Roommate
<u>**www.LeslieNorthBooks.com**</u>

EXCERPT

Chapter one

"Hello, I'm Harley Von." A woman's voice, soft and uncertain, reached Garrett through the open door as he waited in Sebastian's lawyer's office. "I'm here to see Mr. Burke for a will reading."

Garrett sat up a little straighter. So here was the mysterious Harley, just a few feet away and heading toward him. Damn, he wished he weren't meeting Sebastian's sister under these circumstances. Why the hell couldn't Sebastian have lived to welcome her to his home? The fact that he'd never get to reconnect with Harley made his death an even bigger tragedy.

"Yes, hello. He had to step out to take an urgent call, but you can wait in his office," the receptionist said. "He'll be right in. The other party involved is already inside. Can I get you coffee or tea?"

"No, thank you. I'm fine. Through here?" Why did her voice sound so timid? Was she naturally soft-spoken… or had Sebastian been right to think that she was in a bad relationship?

"That's right, honey. Just take a seat."

Garrett stood and turned toward the door, not sure what to expect. Would Harley look like Sebastian? He steeled himself to find out.

Damn, she did. Dark hair, tanned skin, full lips, and wide brown eyes that met his for a second before turning downward. It was long enough for him to recognize those eyes. They were just like Sebastian's—same size, shape, color. But they lacked the warmth and friendship Sebastian's had always held. In their place was a wariness bordering on fear.

Harley was above average height for a woman, but slim, almost too thin. He studied her face. She'd carefully applied makeup, but it looked like she had a bruise near her left eye. His concerns about that relationship ratcheted up.

"Ms. Von," he said. "I'm Garrett Moore. I served with your brother and considered him my closest friend." He held out his hand, and she shook it so quickly that he barely felt the press of her fingers before they were withdrawn. "Maybe you should sit?" He didn't want to order her to, but he feared that if she didn't, she'd either run or faint.

"Thank you. And please, call me Harley." She took the chair next to his, discreetly scooting it a little farther away, and quickly crossed her legs. Long legs that her black skirt showed plenty of. He yanked his eyes away, reminding himself that this wasn't the time or place and definitely not the person he should be noticing in that way. Focusing on her face, he watched as she nervously tucked her long hair behind her ear and then pulled it forward again. Was she trying to conceal the bruise?

"I'm so sorry about your brother," Garrett said.

She gave him a brief glance. "I'm sorry for you, too, if you were his friend. I wish I could have made it to his funeral. I… I wanted to."

"His SEAL team was here. And others who knew him. Do you want to hear about it?" he asked. He didn't want to relive the funeral, but she deserved to hear the details, if she wanted them.

"Please."

He talked for a few minutes about Matthew and Jonathan, the 21-gun salute, and the playing of Taps, making sure to emphasize how respected and loved Sebastian had been. When the lawyer still failed to return, he kept going and told her about Patrick and his wife Imogen, Anderson and Violet, and Kenton and Mia. If Harley was going to stay in Hartsville, she'd want friends, and his fellow SEALs and their wives were a good place to start. He knew they'd be more than happy to step up and help her feel at home.

"Thank you for being there," she said when he was done, and he fought to hide a flinch. She shouldn't thank him. If she knew what had happened, the responsibility he bore for her brother's death, she might curse him. He doubted that, though, since she seemed sweet. He wanted to say the right thing to her, but he didn't know what that was. Before he figured out how to reply, the lawyer entered the room.

"Sorry about that," the man said before stepping over to Harley. "Anthony Burke, attorney at law. You must be Ms. Von?" When she nodded, he reached out to shake her hand. Garrett felt the tiniest bit better when she didn't hold on to the lawyer's hand for any longer than she'd held his. "I'm very sorry for your loss. Thank you for coming all this way for the will reading. I don't want to drag this out.

Dealing with the death of any family member is difficult, but it's even harder when it's so unexpected. Shall we get started?"

"That would be appreciated," Garrett answered for himself and Harley, who only gave a nod.

Burke sat behind his desk and opened a folder. He pulled several papers from it and spread them out. "The terms of Sebastian Valenti's will are pretty straightforward. All SEALs are required to have an updated will on file at the base, but your brother took the additional step of having a signed original here in Hartsville as well."

Garrett cast a glance at Harley. She looked even more fragile than earlier.

"Would you like me to do the official reading or cut through the legal language to provide an overview?" Burke asked.

"Just give me the synopsis, please," she said.

"In short, Sebastian left everything to you, with Garrett Moore as the executor." Burke turned his attention to one page in particular, which appeared to list the assets. "By everything, I mean his home on the lake here in Hartsville—including the boat docked there—his car, the funds in his bank accounts, and his investments. He specifically named an investment that he'd made in a friend's start-up company with the note that he hoped you would continue to support the business."

"Oh," she breathed.

"Here are copies of the most recent bank and investment account statements." He handed over a sheaf of papers.

"I hadn't expected…" She bit her lower lip as she trailed off.

"Your brother was a man who managed his income well." Burke's tone was gentle. "You'll also receive his life insurance and the death benefits from the Navy. All of that is in order." He caught Garrett's eye and nodded to an open box on the edge of his desk. "Mr. Moore, if you'd like to…"

Garrett had placed the box there when he'd first entered the office, so he wasn't surprised at Burke's request. He took the box, knowing that what was in it would be difficult for Harley to see.

"Harley. The Navy gives a flag to the next of kin during a military funeral. I accepted it on your behalf. It's in here along with Sebastian's service medals and official portrait. If you'd rather not look at them now—"

"No, I'd like to," she said, drawing herself up. She still didn't make eye contact with him, but she was staring at the box as if it were the most valuable thing in the world. "I only ever saw him on that one Zoom—I mean, since we were kids—and I can't remember what he looked like clearly. I was only six when we were separated."

Garrett pulled out the portrait taken two years earlier and handed it to her. She studied it carefully for several seconds, running her fingers over the glass. Garrett had many more photographs of Sebastian on his phone. He'd show those to her and tell her stories about her brother before he returned to base, so she could get a better sense of Sebastian. She deserved that.

"There's a note for you as well. It came in an email to me. Would you like me to read it?" the lawyer asked. When she nodded, Burke started with the date: just two weeks before Sebastian's death. He would have already been in Colombia, prepping for the mission.

"'If you're reading this, it means I'm gone. I'm so sorry, Sis. I'd hoped that we'd have more time, that we'd be able to really get to know each other, but it looks like it wasn't meant to be. I want you to know how much it means to me that I finally found you. Please know that I love you, and I've kept you in my heart.'"

Burke paused when Harley let out a soft sob, but she waved for him to continue. Garrett wanted to take her hand and give her what comfort he could, but she didn't look as if she'd welcome being touched.

"'I know that I'm not leaving you alone, since my best friend, Garrett, should be sitting by your side. If you need anything, ask him. I mean that. There's no one in the world I trust more. I hope you have a happy life, Harley. I'm sorry I won't be there to share it. All my love, Sebastian.'"

Garrett felt his friend's words deep in his soul. Sebastian had trusted him, but Garrett had failed him in the end. He hadn't forced Sebastian to join him on that raid, but when he'd volunteered for it, he had known that Sebastian would, as well. They'd always done everything together. If one of them went, the other did, too.

Except now. Garrett was alone, but he could honor Sebastian's memory by helping his sister. He'd do what he could for her.

"Is there anything else?" she asked, seeming anxious to leave the office.

"Just a small delay for you to be aware of. The will has to go through probate, but due to the rotation of the court, we just missed the visit from the circuit court judge. He comes back around to our courthouse in four weeks. I hope that won't be too much of a problem. Garrett has access to the house, as well as the boat and car. You can take immediate possession of those, though you won't be able to sell anything until the estate is settled. The only issue is with the financial accounts. I'm afraid you won't be able to get into those until the judge returns."

"That's fine, as long as I have a place to live for now." She stood. "Thank you both." With that, she took the packet of papers and the box and headed for the door.

Garrett caught up with her on the street as she was getting into an older Buick sedan. "Harley. Wait a minute." She gave him a nervous look as he approached. "You don't know where the house is. I assume you want to go there."

"I do. Isn't the address in the papers?" She was still clutching them.

"Probably, but the roads out by the lake can be confusing if you're not familiar with the town. Why don't you follow me?"

She didn't answer right away as she glanced down the street. Hartsville had an old-fashioned downtown with brick-fronted buildings that housed small businesses. Did she like what she saw here? He did, even if it wasn't home to him. He hoped it would be to her. Being in Hartsville might give her the fresh start he had a feeling she needed.

"Sebastian trusted you. I guess I can, too," she said after a minute, but she didn't sound convinced of it.

Out here in the daylight, it was easier to see past her makeup job to the full, nasty extent of the bruise. It looked to be the kind that happens when someone's fist connects with a face. It was on the tip of his tongue to ask about it, but he didn't know her well enough yet. Despite that, every protective nerve in his body fired at rapid speed. He'd help anyone in trouble, but there was something more about Harley herself that drew Garrett in. He told himself that it was just because she was Sebastian's sister… but deep down, he wondered if it was something more.

Grab your copy of
The SEAL's Pregnant Roommate
www.LeslieNorthBooks.com

BLURB

Retired Navy SEAL, Clint Backwater, enjoys his solitary life as owner of the *Ask Questions Later* gun range. It's the kind of place you find because you know a guy. So when Leila Ortiz, a petite woman with a "baby on board" sticker on the back of her car—and an 18-month-old boy in her arms—shows up at the range, panicked and desperate for a gun, he knows something is wrong. Having grown up in the foster system, Clint has seen what happens when you let yourself get too invested—things get messy, people leave. He made himself a promise to never get emotionally involved again, but the former SEAL in him feels the tug to help this woman and her child.

Leila's ex-husband is being released from prison early on good behavior and she found out too late. He was supposed to serve five years, not two, and Leila is unprepared to protect herself and her son. She promised him they'd never run again—they've made a nice life for themselves and the last thing she wants to do is leave it all behind.

When Clint refuses to give Leila a gun without lessons, she agrees to return to the range to learn. At first, Leila won't say why she's so desperate for protection, but when the threats from her ex escalate, it becomes clear what she's afraid of.

Clint is a loner. Always has been, always will be. So when Leila and her little son enter his life, it hits him—hard— maybe being alone isn't what he needs. Still, having his solitary life disrupted when he invites the little family into his home is a bit tougher to take than he thought. With Leila and her son in danger, though, he'll do whatever it takes to keep them safe—even putting up with stray toys and changing a diaper or two.

But the biggest danger might be to his heart, when it starts to look like the safest thing for Leila and her baby might be to leave her problems —and her budding relationship with Clint—behind.

Grab your copy of *Guarding The Single Mother (SEAL Endgame Book One)* from
www.LeslieNorthBooks.com

EXCERPT

Chapter one

A quiet day on the gun range was a good day on the gun range.

At least that was usually Clint Blackwater's philosophy. Today, though, as he wandered around the small showroom of his business, Ask Questions Later Firearms and Training, he couldn't seem to shake the restlessness inside him.

If he was truthful with himself, he'd have to admit that his skittishness had nothing to do with the slow day at the range and everything to do with the approach of the one-year anniversary of his retirement from the military. Since joining the Navy right out of high school and undergoing training to become a SEAL, he'd always been a busy guy. Busy, but solitary. Relationships weren't really his thing, platonic or otherwise. Loved ones, in Clint's experience, had a tendency to disappear. When he'd been in the military, surrounded by his team and other colleagues every day with privacy at a minimum, he'd thought he'd appreciate the quiet peace of being alone.

Now, though, he was lucky if he talked to six people a day, and sometimes things were a bit too… silent. Not that he was a recluse or anything. It was just living by himself out in the Nevada desert meant his penchant for self-sufficiency came in handy, even if it was lonely at times.

Today, his buddy, Devin, was there to talk to as he checked the inventory of ammunition and firearms and accessories for the umpteenth time. Ask Questions Later provided him with a livable income between the sales of stock and the fees he charged locals for using the gun range and for shooting lessons, but he wouldn't be making the Forbes 500 list any time soon. That was okay. After seeing the worst humanity had to offer during his stint in the SEALs, and prior to that as a kid growing up in the foster care system, Clint was fine with making enough to get by. He didn't need to be rich. He didn't need much of anything—and he liked it that way.

Clint moved from display case to display case, noting the stock in each, while doing his best to ignore Devin chatting loudly on his cell phone. To call the other man a "buddy" was probably being generous. Devin was more like a guy who Clint talked to when he came in to shoot. They sometimes shared a meal at Ritzi's Diner in town. That was about. Still, it was more than Clint did with most folks these days.

He finished up marking down the sixteen boxes of .45 caliber bullets in front of him, then moved to the next glass-topped case, giving Devin some serious side-eye as he did so.

"What do you mean she won't go out with me?" Devin whined into his phone. The guy was pretty typical of the sort who came into the gun range. A wannabe cowboy with a Stetson on his head and a holster strapped around his waist. Nevada tended to be a haven for Mavericks and outlaws, due to the wide-open spaces and the mind-your-own-business attitude of the local law enforcement and residents. It's what led to things like Las Vegas and the Mustang Ranch and dudes like Devin who fancied themselves Billy the Kid reborn. "I'm everything she said she wanted in her online dating profile."

Clint gave a snort and shook his head. Devin was harmless enough. Clint had run into lots of guys like him in the military. Gungho to preserve life, liberty, and the American way—as long as it didn't push them too far out of their comfort zone. But everyone had their own comfort zone, Clint supposed. As a SEAL, he'd been accustomed to facing danger the likes of which most people couldn't imagine. But internet dating, like Devin? Not a chance.

He shuddered at the thought of connecting with a total stranger and trying to make small talk.

The sound of a car door slamming echoed through the quiet store and Clint peered through the sunlight streaming through the glass front door. Outside, a dust-covered black SUV had pulled up. Or backed up, would be more accurate. Through the hazy glass he saw a "Baby on Board" sticker in the back window.

Probably another local dad wanting some away time from his wife and kids.

Clint turned to head back behind the counter. He'd just about made it when he heard Devin behind him saying, "Uh, I think my dream girl just pulled into my life."

Cringing, Clint gave his buddy a disgusted look over the corny line and was just about to rib him about it when the bells above the door jingled and in walked said girl.

Or woman, to be more accurate. A woman with a baby.

Huh. Okay. Clint narrowed his gaze a bit, focusing on her as she stepped closer and moved out of the stream of light that silhouetted her from behind. Twenty-five, he'd guess, so about ten years younger than him. Wavy dark hair, golden bronzed skin. Large dark eyes that were scanning the shop nervously.

She's scared.

The thought hit Clint out of nowhere, considering he'd never seen her before in his life, but he'd bet his business and everything he owned that he was right. His instincts had been honed on the battlefield, and retirement hadn't dulled them. After all, you couldn't afford to get careless when you owned a gun shop.

His conclusions were only confirmed as she moved closer to the front counter and met his gaze. There were shadows in those pretty brown eyes of hers, deep and dark and dangerous. Then there was the fact her nails looked chewed to the quick and her hands shook slightly as she bounced her cute baby in one arm. A boy, from what he could tell from the blue jeans and baseball hat on the kid's head. Maybe a year, year and a half old, Clint guessed.

"Welcome to Ask Questions Later Firearms and Training," he said, his words emerging a bit rougher than usual because of the odd constriction in this throat. Not nervousness. Not adrenaline. Attraction. Clint swallowed hard and crossed his arms. "How can I help you today?"

The woman took a deep breath and checked behind her once more before saying quietly, "I need to buy a gun."

∾

Oh God.

The last place Leila Ortiz ever thought she'd find herself was in a gun store. She wasn't an aggressive or confrontational person by nature. Just the opposite in fact. But circumstances—and the fact that the Federal Bureau of Prisons had screwed up her contact information—meant that she and her son needed protection in a major way, and they needed it ASAP.

She eyed the man behind the counter and did her best to look as confident as possible. She couldn't match his defensive posture, not with Thomas in her arms, but she could mimic that blank, closed-off stare he was giving her. "I've heard that Glocks are good for women to use. I'd like to see one of those, please."

"A Glock, huh?" The guy narrowed his gaze on her then stepped forward. Leila stepped back automatically before she stopped herself. Years of abuse had taught her it was easier to retreat than to stand her ground, but that had all changed the day Thomas had been born. Now she had more than herself to think about. Now she had her son to protect. He looked her up and down. Not in a sexual way, more in a what-the-heck-are-you-doing-in-here way. She checked him out too, again out of habit. If attacked it was best to have a good description for the cops. Short, light brown hair. Blue eyes. Maybe five-ten, five-eleven max, with a muscular build. A hint of a tattoo on his left bicep peeked out from beneath the sleeve of his dark blue T-shirt—a snake perhaps, wrapped around a knife? Weird.

Leila shook off her errant thoughts about the man. She didn't care if this dude had Daffy Duck and Wily Coyote inked all over himself. She needed a gun and fast. Her ex was coming back to town and no way would she allow him anywhere near her or their son. He'd lost his parental privileges the day he'd beat her up so badly she'd ended up in the ER with two broken ribs and a bruised collarbone. That had been the same night she'd discovered she was pregnant with Thomas. Talk about the good with the bad. She stepped up to the counter once more and set Thomas atop of it. He was eighteen-months old now and weighed nearly twenty-five pounds. Good for Thomas, not so good for her when she had to hold him for extended lengths of time. Leila was strong, but her usual workouts had not prepared her for handling a squirming kid in her arms for hours at a time.

"Unless you think there's another firearm that might work better for me," she said, doing her best to focus on the important conversation at hand and not the fact that her baby was currently grinning and cooing at the man behind the counter. "I don't really care as long as it works."

The guy placed the heels of his hands against the glass topped case and rested his weight on them. His movement caused his muscles to ripple beneath his T-shirt. Not that she was noticing. Nope. After a lifetime of bad experiences with men, Leila was done with them. Well, except for Thomas. But she'd raise him right. Raise him to respect women and not yell at them or hit them. She'd had quite enough of that from her father growing up and later from her ex. If only she'd known he'd been involved with a gang—running drugs and worse— she'd never have married him. But she'd been young and stupid, and she'd given him her heart and her virginity at twenty-two thinking he'd take her away to a better life. He'd taken her away all right. Straight to hell. Now, three years later, she was alone and raising her son as best she could.

No way would Mike ever get near them again. No. Way.

"You ever used a gun before?" the guy asked, his tone dripping with suspicion.

"No." Leila raised her chin. "But it can't be that hard, right? Point and shoot."

"Not exactly." The guy glanced over her shoulder and the hair on the back of her neck prickled. Shit. Someone else was in the store. She'd vaguely registered another person when she'd entered but had been so focused on getting a weapon she hadn't paid much attention. *Stupid, Leila. So stupid.* The first thing they'd taught her in those self-defense classes she'd taken last year had been to be aware of your surroundings at all times.

She turned fast, one hand on Thomas on the counter, the other clutching her keys between her fingers, ready to lash out at whoever tried to hurt her.

"Whoa there, little lady," a skinny guy in a cowboy hat said, holding up his hands in surrender. "Didn't mean to startle you. I was just going to ask you if you wanted to get a cup of coffee."

"She doesn't want coffee, Dev," the guy behind the counter answered for her.

"How do you know what I want?" Leila frowned at him and squinted at the name embroidered on the man's T-shirt. "Clint."

"*Do* you want coffee?" He raised a brow at her.

No, she didn't. But it was none of his business and she didn't need him talking over her and answering her questions. "What I want is a gun. You going to sell me one or not?"

"Not without a background check and proof you've had the proper training."

Damn. It wasn't that she couldn't pass the check, but she had no training. Nor did she have a license for that matter. Leila shook her head. She'd not really thought things through before racing down here. She'd always been a bit impulsive that way, as her mother would attest. It's what had gotten her in trouble with her father growing up, always doing things without considering the consequences. It was how she'd ended up married to an abusive asshole like her ex. It was the main thing that kept her up at night wondering how in the world she'd ever be a fit mother for poor Thomas. If she couldn't make good choices for herself, how would she ever be able to do that for her child?

"Dev, go away," the guy behind the counter said, his voice authoritative. "Go find yourself another online girlfriend and leave this lady alone." Surprisingly, the other man did as he was told, the bells over the door jangling merrily at his departure. That left her alone with Mr. Intense, Cute, and Brooding. He focused those bright blue eyes of his on her again and squinted. "Perhaps if you tell me what you need the gun for, I can figure out what would work best for you."

"Oh." She tucked her hair behind her ear and pulled a leather key chain from a nearby display away from Thomas before he drooled all over it. "Just the usual. Can't be too careful these days."

"Look. I can tell you're nervous about something. I don't mean to pry, but if you're in trouble in some way, maybe I can help. I used to be in the military and—"

The tension inside Leila exploded into full-blown panic. The fewer people who knew about her past and her ex, the better. She'd come in here on the recommendation of a friend, expecting quick service and no questions. Wasn't that what the business's name seemed to promise? This wasn't what she wanted. It was bad enough she was even in here, trying to buy a gun. Blood pounding in her head and pulse racing, Leila picked up Thomas and headed for the exit. "I need to go. Sorry. I'll come back later."

**Grab your copy of *Guarding The Single Mother (SEAL Endgame Book One)* from
www.LeslieNorthBooks.com**